"Thank you for the offer..."

"But?"

Teresa shook her head. "No buts, well, maybe a small one. I am just going to wait until they contact me again, making demands for the money."

He leaned forward, his mouth so close to hers that she could smell his sweet, minty breath, count the individual hairs in his scruffy beard, see the small scar on his bottom lip. God, she wanted him to kiss her, to take her to bed, away from thoughts of debt and mobsters and inheritances she didn't want.

Teresa lifted her hand and rubbed her thumb against his bottom lip, surprised at how soft his lips were.

Liam pulled the tip of her thumb between his teeth and bit down gently.

God, was he ever going to kiss her?

* * *

Redeemed by Passion is part of the Dynasties: Secrets of the A-List series.

Dear Reader,

It was such a joy to write the final book of the Dynasties: Secrets of The A-List series. Working with my fellow Desire authors Cat Schield, Karen Booth and Reese Ryan was a wonderful experience. While this book is a stand-alone, your reading pleasure will be enhanced if you read their books in the series.

In *Redeemed by Passion*, I pick up Liam Christopher and Teresa St. Claire's story, which was detailed in the other books. Liam and Teresa are attracted to each other, but my fellow authors threw obstacle after obstacle in their path. I do, too.

Teresa is an event coordinator and Liam is a billionaire businessman, but they both bring a mountain of baggage to their relationship. He's not sure of his parentage, and she has a brother who causes mayhem in her life. There is also someone in the shadows who is determined to destroy Teresa by any means possible.

Can they find their happily-ever-after, with or without The Fixer's interference?

Read on to find out!

Happy reading,

Joss

Connect with me at www.josswoodbooks.com

Twitter: @josswoodbooks

Facebook: Joss Wood Author

JOSS WOOD

———

REDEEMED BY PASSION

HARLEQUIN®DESIRE

Special thanks and acknowledgment are
given to Joss Wood for her contribution to
the Dynasties: Secrets of the A-List series.

PLEASE RECYCLE
THIS PRODUCT IS RECYCLABLE

ISBN-13: 978-1-335-60381-4

Recycling programs
for this product may
not exist in your area.

Redeemed by Passion

HARLEQUIN®
www.Harlequin.com

Printed in U.S.A.

Joss Wood loves books and traveling—especially to the wild places of Southern Africa and, well, anywhere. She's a wife, a mom to two teenagers and slave to two cats. After a career in local economic development, she now writes full-time. Joss is a member of Romance Writers of America and Romance Writers of South Africa.

Books by Joss Wood

Harlequin Desire

The Ballantyne Billionaires

His Ex's Well-Kept Secret
One Night to Forever
The CEO's Nanny Affair
Little Secrets: Unexpectedly Pregnant

Love in Boston

Friendship on Fire
Hot Christmas Kisses
The Rival's Heir

Dynasties: Secrets of the A-List

Redeemed by Passion

Visit her Author Profile page at Harlequin.com, or josswoodbooks.com, for more titles.

You can find Joss Wood on Facebook, along with other Harlequin Desire authors, at Facebook.com/harlequindesireauthors!

One

Liam Christopher tipped his head up and tracked the winking light of a jet above him. That could, for all he knew, be Brooks Abbingdon's jet carrying Teresa away from him. The image of Teresa curled up in Brooks's lap, him comforting her as she cried—because, hell, if anyone deserved to cry it was Teresa St. Claire—flashed on his retina and his grip tightened on the crystal tumbler in his hand. He heard a sharp crack and a second later, expensive liquor ran over his palm and under the wristband of his watch.

Liam opened his hand and looked at the cracked glass and its sharp shards. Surprisingly, there was no blood. Transferring the broken glass from his hand to the coffee table on the balcony, he shook the droplets of his Manhattan cocktail off his hand before reaching for his pocket square and wiping the liquid away.

Well, that was a waste of good booze. Liam looked back into the luxurious Presidential Suite of the Goblet Hotel and saw his friend Matt Richmond pacing the area between the designer sofas and the dining table. Matt was pissed and he had a right to be. His gala evening was ruined and would be long remembered for all the wrong reasons.

And it was all Teresa's fault. Well, not her fault exactly—she hadn't known that her brother would show up and ruin months of work—but as the event planner, the buck stopped with her.

Would her company recover from this? He doubted it. Would she? Teresa was tough but she'd had a couple of hard knocks lately. When Matt asked her to leave the retreat immediately, taking her brother with her, Teresa knew that her reputation was about to take another beating, and Liam understood why she felt the need to run. Why would she want to stay and witness the pitying looks, the cruel smirks, hear the caustic comments?

She also wanted to run from him. And that, he understood most of all.

Seeing movement in the room behind him, Liam turned his head to watch Nadia approach Matt, her eyes on her man. Matt was still on the phone but he held out his hand and Nadia tucked herself into his side, her arms encircling his waist. Matt dropped a kiss on her head before continuing his conversation. Liam's stomach cramped with what he thought might be jealousy. He'd never believed in true love—hadn't been exposed to it growing up—but maybe it did exist; maybe it was just as rare as hell. Matt had found his Holy Grail in Nadia but Liam wasn't naive enough to believe that everybody, most especially him, would be that lucky.

Love, he was convinced, wasn't for him.

Matt threw his phone onto the sofa behind him and pulled his wife into his body, burying his face in the crook of her neck. Although Nadia was a foot shorter than Matt, Liam knew that he was sucking strength from her, that Matt was leaning on her. They were a unit, taking turns to lead and to follow, to give and receive strength. They were two trees growing together, sharing soil and water, their branches and roots intermingling.

It struck him that he and Teresa were two separate pine trees planted in a regimented row. They both stood tall, took the wind, never bent. They'd been planted too far apart—and too much had happened between them and to them—to bridge the gap to be able to even start to explore anything deeper than flash point sex.

Liam turned away and walked to the edge of the balcony, gripping the balustrade with tight fingers. Maybe Teresa's leaving, her breaking it off for good, was—as she'd said—what was best for her, him, Christopher Corporation. For everybody involved.

And if that was true then why did he feel like week-old crap?

Hearing Matt's footsteps he turned his head and

saw Matt approaching him, a bottle of bourbon in his hand. Matt raised his eyebrows at the broken glass and, without words, handed Liam the bottle. Liam took a hefty sip before dropping the bottle to his side, holding it in a loose grip. By the time dawn broke, he was going to be best buds with this bottle.

"Where's Nadia?"

Matt leaned his butt against the railing and rolled his head from side to side to release the knots in his neck. Liam didn't bother; his knots were now permanent residents. "She went to bed," Matt replied. He glanced at his watch. "It is almost three in the morning."

"It was a hell of a night." Liam took another hit from the bottle, ignoring his still-sticky hand. He glanced up, saw another jet and forced himself to meet Matt's eyes. "I feel like I should apologize."

"For what?" Matt asked, his eyes and tone weary. "You didn't cause Teresa's brother to ruin my gala evening."

"Neither did Teresa," Liam responded, needing to defend her.

"Tell me about her brother," Matt said, moving to the sofa and dropping down. He immediately tucked a pillow under his head and propped his feet up onto the coffee table.

Ordinarily, Liam would never consider divulging someone else's secrets but this was Matt, his best friend, and he trusted him implicitly. He also needed Matt's sharp brain to help him make sense of what was, at this crazy hour, the senseless.

"It's a tangled mess but I'm going to tell you what I do know, gathered from what Teresa has told me, along with what my investigator dug up.

"So years ago, Joshua, her brother, liked drugs and alcohol a little too much and got himself in debt with some unsavory characters. They offered him a job to pay off the money. He became a chauffeur—"

"And he, knowingly or unknowingly, ferried drugs," Matt finished for him.

Matt was, by far, the sharpest tool in the shed. "Yep. He was busted and was jailed. Via Mariella Santiago-Marshall, Teresa employed the talents of The Fixer—"

Matt whistled his astonishment. "I've heard of him. He's—"

Liam raised an eyebrow. "Effective?"

"I was going to say *ruthless* but that works, too."

"Anyway," Liam continued, "he got Joshua's charges dropped, him out of jail and across the country. The kid didn't learn and has raked up another huge gambling debt. A mafia-type organization has bought that debt from the original crew and it's rocketed to an impossible sum."

"How much?"

"Seven million dollars," Liam replied. "Several weeks back Teresa was told that he'd been kidnapped but that turned out to be BS. Teresa's been informed that she needs to repay his loan, but she doesn't have that kind of cash, and they've never called her back, as far as I know."

"Pay it for her, offset it against the cost of the

shares you are going to buy from her when she's completed her yearlong mandatory stint on the board of Christopher Corporation," Matt suggested. "As per the terms of your father's will."

"Teresa is hoping that she can delay repaying them until she's sold her shares. She wants to keep me out of the equation. Hell, maybe she's shopping around for a better deal for the shares." The thought of Teresa selling those shares to anyone else made his stomach whirl. If she did that, he would no longer have the thin sliver of control over Christopher Corporation he did now.

"Nobody has given Teresa, or Joshua, a firm deadline for the repayment of the debt."

"Weird," Matt agreed. "So it should be imperative that he keep his head down, even stay out of sight. Then why would Joshua crash a highly visible, live-streamed event?

"What does Teresa think?" Matt asked, after a moment's silence.

"I don't know since she blew me off and hightailed it back to Seattle in Abbingdon's private plane," Liam muttered his sour reply. He pulled his cell out of his pocket and hit the speed dial number that would connect him to Teresa. It didn't mean anything that he'd moved his personal assistant, Duncan, to number two on his list and Teresa to number one. It meant nothing. At all.

Liam listened to her phone ring and urged her to pick up. He needed to know that she was okay, that Joshua was okay—God, the kid hadn't looked, or sounded, good. And he wasn't talking about the bruise his fist made on his jaw. Her phone went to voice mail and he dropped a hard "Call me" order into her message system.

Liam placed the bourbon bottle on the coffee table, sat down in the chair opposite Matt and rested his forearms on his knees. He released a series of low but intense f-bombs.

"That kind of sums up my feelings about this evening," Matt commented. "I've been doing damage control but there's not much spin you can generate when everything is caught on video and then livestreamed."

Liam winced. "How many views?"

"Far too many." Matt lifted his glass in a sarcastic salute. "I've got to admit, when Teresa messes up, she does it properly."

"She didn't know her brother was in town, never mind that he was going to do that," Liam retorted.

"So defending her seems to be your default reaction tonight," Matt commented, hitting the nail on its head.

Liam sent his best friend a hard stare. "What's your point, Matt?"

"It's been one drama after another with her, starting with the fact that you thought she had an affair with your dad."

"She explained that. My father was her mentor and good friend."

Matt rolled his eyes. "They had to be very good

friends for him to leave Teresa a twenty-five-percent stake in Christopher Corporation worth millions."

When Matt put it like that, all his fears and insecurities about their relationship floated to the surface. Was he being conned? Could he believe Teresa's version of what happened? In his final hours, Linus did confirm that there had been nothing between them but friendship and Liam wanted to believe him, them. But he'd been raised to believe that everyone lied so how the hell could he trust anything they said? Anything anybody said?

He thought he could, at least, trust his parents to some degree but their latest lie had been the biggest of his life. As his father lay dying, he realized that it was scientifically impossible that his parents, with their blood groups, could produce a child with his blood group. Ergo, either only one of them was his biological parent or he was adopted. Hell of a thing to realize at the age of thirty-two.

Was it any wonder he was so messed up when it came to relationships?

It was late and Liam was done with talking. He wanted this conversation to end so he told Matt that Teresa wanted nothing more to do with him. Liam caught the look of relief on Matt's face. "You're happy about that?"

Matt shook his head. "*Happy* is the wrong word…" He sat up, swinging his feet off the table. "It's just that relationships shouldn't be this hard, bud. Over the past few months you've thought that she's a liar, a gold digger and an opportunist. You've slept with her and then slept with other women."

No, he hadn't. "I tried to sleep with someone else to get her out of my system."

Matt waved his explanation away. "Whatever. She hit the tabloids, dragging you along with her. Those scum-suckers informed the world that she had an affair with your father and that she only slept with Linus to get her hands on the company."

He knew this. He'd goddamn lived it. "Do you have a point and are you going to get to it in the near future?"

"My point is that, while I actually like Teresa—"

"You could've fooled me." Liam's interjection was bone-dry.

"I do like her," Matt said. "She's smart, super-organized and she's an amazing event planner. Yeah, I'm mad as hell that tonight ended the way it did, but intellectually, I get that it wasn't her fault. But her career did not need this and if she was boycotted before, it's going to be nothing like what's going to happen to her now."

Liam gripped the bridge of his nose. God.

Matt's long sigh was audible. "But at the end of the day, my loyalty is to you. And, as your friend, I am telling you that I don't think she is good for you because, frankly, you look like crap."

Well, that wasn't news.

"Are you in love with her?"

Liam's head shot up and his eyes slammed into Matt's. His throat closed as panic crept up. In his sappier moments lately, he'd flirted with the idea of love, but that was just a result of hormones and stupendous sex. No, of course he wasn't in love with Teresa; he didn't believe in love. But he was attracted to her, stupidly so. And attraction was easily confused for that other emotion. He croaked a "No."

Matt stood up and gripped his shoulder. "Can I then just point out that this woman you profess not to love has the innate ability to mess with your head and your life? That's an enormous amount of power for someone you just like to sleep with."

Craphelldammit.

"Go to bed, Matt."

Matt smiled for the first time that evening. "Yep, that's where I'm heading. Into the arms of the woman who, instead of messing with my head and life, actually makes my life better and brighter."

Liam glared at his friend as he walked back into the hotel room and thought about returning to his own suite, to the empty king-size bed waiting for him. But the night was mild, this sofa was quite comfortable and he had a bottle to keep him company. And really, he had too much on his mind to sleep.

Liam lay back and tucked a pillow under his head and watched the light of airplanes move between the stars.

Right, exactly what level of hell had she reached? Teresa St. Claire had experienced hot—Liam Christopher believing that she'd had an affair with his father—and knew what blistering felt like when her face was plastered over the front pages of the tabloid press accusing her of stealing Liam's fortune.

But tonight she'd stood inside the flames, her skin melting.

Now, as Brooks Abbingdon's jet cut through the dark night, Teresa felt frozen, her heart encased in dry ice. Maybe true hell was this dead-on-the-inside, will-never-recover feeling.

Teresa flopped down into the chair opposite Brooks Abbingdon and eyed her brother through half-closed eyes. A bright blue bruise colored his jaw, and his lower lip was swollen. She loved Joshua, but right now she didn't like him even a little bit. The only man she felt remotely charitable toward was Brooks Abbingdon, who'd offered her a ride out of the nightmare that was her latest professional disaster zone. He was also sitting across from her, ankle on his knee, deep in thought.

Teresa swallowed down a groan and felt her stomach cramp. Her reputation, along with her company, had been dancing on the knife-edge of ruin for weeks but her brother gate-crashing her most illustrious clients' gala evening and, worse, grabbing the mic from singer Jessie Humphrey and placing himself front and center while ranting about rich losers and liars had pushed her off that sliver-thin edge.

And since she would be, if she wasn't already, person very non grata by morning, why had Brooks Abbingdon, CEO of Abbingdon Airlines, rushed to her rescue? He was rich, successful and gorgeous so she had no idea why he'd offered them a lift on his plane heading back to Seattle. But she wasn't complaining; she needed to get Joshua back under the radar as soon as possible and Brooks had offered her a way out.

Joshua was hunched over in his seat, mumbling to himself. Thank God he'd stopped ranting, his words and sentences not making any sense.

Teresa couldn't pull her eyes off his face. Joshua had been a pain in her ass, especially these past few years, but he was her baby brother; she'd always looked after him. Initially, she'd blamed his actions on a combination of drugs and alcohol, but earlier she'd touched his left arm and he'd cried out. Teresa rolled back his sleeveshirt to see a small but distinctive puncture mark on his forearm. In a place where it would be difficult for him to self-inject. Like so much else about this night, nothing made sense.

But hell, why was she surprised? This was her insane life; everything and anything was possible.

Teresa looked from Joshua to Brooks and found his eyes studying her. Teresa waited for the kick of attraction, for a spark, and sighed when nothing happened. Maybe she wasn't responding to him because she was exhausted and overwrought because Brooks was everything she normally found attractive in a man. At six-four or so, he was tall but perfectly proportioned with wide shoulders, narrow hips and long, muscular legs. His voice, carrying the accent of an expensive British education, was deep and luscious, his face masculine and sexy, and his skin the color of old sepia photographs.

But he wasn't, dammit, Liam.

Gah!

As if she'd summoned him, Teresa heard the discreet beep of her phone and there was his name, flashing on the screen. Her heart whimpered and her stomach clenched. Nope, she couldn't talk to him, not tonight, possibly never again. For the past few months, since she'd stumbled back into his orbit, she'd felt off-kilter and was constantly uncertain about what she'd face on any given day. She'd been a duck, serene on the outside but paddling like hell under the water. As a result, she was utterly drained on just about every level. Tonight she'd bled out every pint of energy she'd ever possessed.

Teresa simply did not know if she'd be able to pick her head up, struggle on. Curling up in a ball and weeping sounded far more fun than fighting another day.

She was done. Possibly for good.

Brooks cleared his throat and Teresa lifted her head to see him holding out a tumbler of whiskey. Taking the glass, she glanced at Joshua. He'd fallen asleep, his head between the edge of the seat and the wall of the plane. Tossing back her whiskey, she lowered the glass and met Brooks's sympathetic eyes.

"Would you like another?" Brooks asked, his words holding the snap of Eton and Oxford.

Teresa shook her head. "If I do, I'll collapse in a heap and then you will have two St. Claires to deal with."

Teresa blew out her breath and gestured to Joshua. "I am *so* sorry. I know I'm repeating myself, but I don't know how he found out where I was working or what prompted him to—" She hesitated, looking for words. *Destroy my career? Embarrass the hell out of me? Bankrupt my business?* "—do what he did."

Brooks lifted his shoulder in a quick shrug. When he didn't respond, Teresa took a deep breath and bit the bullet. "I will absolutely understand if you want to rescind your offer to have me plan your wedding."

Brooks stared at her for a long time and Teresa resisted the urge to squirm. She wouldn't blame him if he pulled his offer for her to plan his wedding; he'd floated the offer earlier that evening, back at the gala, before her carefully planned event went to hell on horseback.

Unbidden, snapshots of the evening jumped onto the big screen of her mind. Joshua ripping the microphone from Jessie's hand, his incoherent screaming. Liam, bigger and stronger than her lanky brother, tackling him to the ground, his fist connecting with Joshua's face. And all of it streaming live to Jessie's fans around the world.

Teresa placed her hand on her heart and tried to rub the pain away. But nope, it wasn't going anywhere.

Brooks tapped a long finger against the Waterford tumbler and shook his head. "Up until your brother's unfortunate interruption, the gala evening, and the weekend, was going well. I'm intelligent enough to see how much work you put into the preparations and how dedicated you are to your job. What he did wasn't your fault."

At the unexpected vote of support, Teresa felt her eyes sting. "Thank you."

"Let's discuss my wedding."

Teresa frowned. It was close to three in the morning, she was exhausted and, after a crappy evening, Brooks wanted her to talk flowers and food? Teresa slapped back her frustration. He was offering her a lifeboat as she treaded water in a stormy sea.

Okay, then. She'd talk weddings. "Sure."

Then she realized that she had no idea who Brooks was marrying and, come to think of it, was still surprised to hear of his engagement. She'd pegged him as a confirmed bachelor, someone who wasn't interested in settling down. She pulled a smile up onto her face. "Who's the lucky lady?"

Brooks stared at her for a moment, his eyes not leaving hers. "You will be informed in due course."

Okay, then. That was a super-weird response. Teresa worked hard not to show her shock, to react in any way other than polite acquiescence. Why the secrecy? Wasn't the bride supposed to be part of these discussions? What was going on here?

Her thoughts scrambling, Teresa linked her hands around her knees and tried to corral her thoughts. Right, moving on. "Do you have a preference on where you would like to marry? When? How many guests? What's your budget?"

Brooks held her eyes when he dropped what Teresa hoped would be the last bombshell of the evening. "You have an unlimited budget and I'm offering to pay double your normal fee."

"What's the catch?" she asked, not sure that she wanted to know.

Brooks smiled. "I need you to organize the wedding of the year so that it can take place on the thirtieth."

"Of what month?" She needed at least six months to prepare; six months was tight but doable.

Brooks held her eye and didn't flinch. "I'm getting married on the last Saturday of this month, Teresa."

Two weeks?

Frick.

Teresa held out her glass and nodded to the whiskey bottle. "Can I have another? And, respectfully, are you insane? There is no way I can plan a wedding in two weeks."

Brooks pulled out his phone and dialed. "She said she can't do it," he said to the person on the other line. He then handed her the phone. "He wants to talk to you."

Two

There was a method to his madness…and a madness to his methods. Shakespeare's quote, Brooks Abbingdon thought, had never been more apt. His particular method of madness was to marry.

In two weeks' time.

Teresa hung up the phone and looked at him with wide, defeated eyes. "I'd be…" she hesitated "…happy to do your wedding. Two weeks is no problem."

Another success for The Fixer and that meant that another hefty bill would be landing in his Brooks's inbox soon. Fact: sometimes you had to pay for things to go your way.

Seeing that Teresa was at the end of her rope— it was the early hours of the morning and she'd had a hell of a day—Brooks told her to rest and Teresa immediately dropped her head back and closed her eyes. She'd been shocked by his time frame; hearing that he had yet to choose a bride might cause her brain to explode.

Because, really, who planned a wedding without securing a bride?

Apparently, he did.

Brooks stretched out his legs and jammed his hands into the pockets of his suit pants, mostly to hide the small tremor in his fingers. Married? Him? He'd always believed, still did, that wedding rings were the world's smallest, strongest pair of handcuffs. But here he was, about to get hitched because his grandfather refused to listen to reason.

Stubborn old bastard.

Lester Abbingdon desperately wanted to invest in a friend's yet-to-be-developed chain of luxury boutique hotels. Brooks wasn't convinced that the investment would provide a decent, or any, return. But Lester rather fancied the idea of being the world's next hotel mogul and, since he couldn't take money from the swimming-in-cash Abbingdon Trust, he was determined to raise the money he needed by selling his personal stake in Abbingdon Airlines. Brooks had no intention of dealing with a new partner, of having to justify his decisions or, far worse, ask for permission to do what he wanted, when he wanted, with his company.

No, the only option was to buy his grandfather's shares from him and in order to raise the cash needed—without having to get banks or other investors involved—that meant, *yippee-doo-dah*, getting married.

Brooks stared out the window into the inky blackness and remembered his first visit to the stuffy offices of the Abbingdon Trust's lawyers. He'd been twenty-one and in their wood-paneled offices, they told him that, as the only Abbingdon heir, he was entitled to a sizeable monthly income from the trust but he was also set to inherit a crap-ton of cash on his twenty-fifth birthday. *If* he was married.

The offer would only be renewed every five years and at twenty-five, using Lester's money to buy his first two cargo planes, he'd opted not to marry—he'd been having too much fun playing the field and had no intention, and no need, to sacrifice his freedom. Ditto at thirty but at thirty-five, Abbingdon Airlines was worth the inconvenience. He wanted control and for control he needed cash; to get the cash he needed to marry...

He'd established and grown Abbingdon Airlines; it was his hard work that had made the company one of the most trusted and respected companies in the country. His clients knew that they could rely on him to get them, or their goods, where they needed to go in the shortest time possible. But Lester wanted to go and play Monopoly with real-life assets and had placed him between a rock and a hard place. Shouldn't ninety-year-old men be smoking cigars and playing bridge?

And of course, every time they spoke about this deal, Lester never failed to remind him that he was ecstatic that he was being forced to marry and that maybe, God willing, he'd get a much-desired great-grandchild, preferably a grandson, out of the deal. Lester then launched into his oft-repeated lecture on his lack of commitment to providing an heir to continue the Abbingdon line, that if he didn't hop to it—his words—six hundred years of DNA-soaked history would cease to exist. The art and furniture collected over twenty-four generations would scatter to private collectors all over the world. Abbingdon Castle and its surrounding land would be sold to the highest bidder. The Abbingdons weren't royalty but they were damn close.

And it all rested on Brooks's shoulders…

Or in his loins.

He'd have a kid, one day. Not now. Right now all he wanted to do was save his company.

Brooks took a sip of his whiskey, staring past young Joshua St. Claire—sleeping now, thank God—to the inky night beyond the window of his Global 7000 jet. The kid was so out of it, he barely registered that he was on a private jet and hadn't noticed the rich leather seats, the fine wood veneers and the stylish carpets and stonework. This jet had just hit the market but he owned one and, being aviation crazy, it annoyed him that neither of his two guests appreciated their luxurious mode of transport.

And his annoyance had nothing to do with the aircraft's hefty price tag, which was upward of half a billion dollars. This plane was superbly designed, exquisitely manufactured and brilliantly engineered.

It was, in its way, a masterpiece. And his guests, like his grandfather, didn't share his passion for anything with an engine and two wings.

His business was damn good. And his life, up until two weeks ago, had been friggin' amazing.

Yet, here he was, planning his wedding. And because the Abbingdon Trust paid for all Abbingdon weddings, he was going to take full advantage and turn his wedding into a massive networking event, inviting all his present clients and anybody he thought could be a potential client. If he was going to put his head in a hangman's noose, then he was going to swing in style.

All he now needed was a bride.

Brooks looked at the cool beauty in the chair across from him and cocked his head. Teresa St. Claire was beautiful; there was no doubt about it. Tall and slim, she rocked an old-school Grace Kelly vibe, classy as hell. Despite the rumors and gossip swirling around her she'd held her head high and he'd yet to see her unhinged, to break into a sweat.

He liked calm women, women who could keep it together when their lives were falling apart. That showed a strength of character few women—hell, few men—possessed. Teresa St. Claire was beautiful, sexy and smart. What more could he want in a wife? The Fixer had also suggested her as a candidate to be his wife; said that she was a possibility and that he could, possibly, make that happen.

Marrying Teresa would've been an elegant, and quick, resolution to his current problem. Except for the

little problem that she was crazy about Liam Christopher... He wasn't the most perceptive guy in the world
but even he noticed the way she looked at Christopher. Part exasperation, part denial, part annoyance
but mostly like all she wanted to do was strip him
naked and do several things to him that were X-rated.
Brooks knew that he was marrying for convenience,
as a means to an end, but he certainly didn't need to
watch his wife pine for someone else. Or wish he was
someone else.

So he refused The Fixer's offer and settled for his
arranging for Teresa to organize his blowout wedding.

What could The Fixer have on her to (a) think that
he could get her to agree to marriage and (b) to get
her to undertake such a massive event on such short
notice? It had to be something...

But Teresa's past didn't concern him and he had
bigger worries. Like who might say yes to his crazy-
ass proposal to marry him.

In two weeks' time.

Happy bloody birthday to him.

Teresa leaned back in her chair and stared out the
high-arched windows of her waterfront office in Seattle, just a few blocks from Pike Market. She loved
her view, her open-plan office with its high ceilings,
industrial lighting and its hardwood floors. But today
all she could think about was the look of betrayal on
Joshua's face as she left him at the tightly controlled
and monitored rehab facility two hours away. He understood that he had to lie low but, damn, his tightly

crossed arms and the emotion washing in and out of his eyes nearly dropped her to her knees.

She wanted to believe his denials about his addictions, she really did. But she still didn't know how to explain that small puncture mark on his arm. Had someone injected him and then, in his woozy and hazy state, manipulated him to take a flight across the country to Napa to gate-crash Matt's party? Was that possible or was she overreacting, allowing her imagination to run wild because she so badly wanted to believe him?

All her anxiety about Joshua would simply evaporate if she could pay off Joshua's debt. Then they'd both be free. She'd been such a naive fool to believe that when the drug-running charges against Joshua were dropped—thanks to The Fixer—he would get his life together. Silly her.

Most women in their late twenties were concerned about their careers, their young children or their new marriages—and, frequently, a combination of all three—but no, she spent her time stressing about unpaid debts to criminals, her inconvenient attraction to a man who blew hot and cold but whom she couldn't avoid, and rocketing from crisis to crisis. It was times like these that Teresa wished she had a mother to turn to but her mom, like her brother, relied on her. Since her father's death, she'd been the glue holding their family together, the strong one, the capable one, the one who could always make a plan.

It would be so nice to rely on someone else, to have someone in her corner loving and supporting her but she was terrified that that person would, just like her father had, fade on her. Sharing the load meant opening up, allowing herself to be vulnerable, exposing herself...

What if that person left, disappeared on her, leaving her to waft in the wind? No, it was better to hang tough...

Besides, there was only one person who'd scaled her walls to peek inside her soul—she hadn't told anyone else but Liam about Joshua and the stress she was under—and he was even more closed up and messed up than she was. They were a hell of a pair...

Teresa heard a throat clear and lifted her head to see Corinne hovering by her partly open door as if deciding whether to knock or not. Teresa dropped her hands, swallowed her sigh and gestured her assistant inside. Corinne's face reflected the grim mood of the rest of her colleagues: they were worried about the future of Limitless Events, and Teresa didn't blame them. For any event company, Saturday's events would be a death knell and she had no doubt that most of her people were brushing up their résumés.

Teresa gestured for Corinne to sit. When Corinne's eyes met hers, she saw her curiosity and knew a dozen questions were hovering on Corinne's tongue. Teresa's respect for her increased when Corinne just powered up her iPad and asked a simple question. "So, what's the plan?"

Teresa tucked a strand of hair that had fallen from her loose bun behind her ear. "The plan is that we arrange Brooks Abbingdon's big blowout wedding."

Corinne's brown eyes widened. "He's getting married? To whom?" Corinne read the social pages and entertainment magazines with utter dedication and Teresa knew that she was wondering whether she'd missed a crucial piece of gossip.

"He didn't say."

Corinne looked at her like she was, finally, losing it. "I'm sorry? I don't understand."

Yep, crazy. "Brooks didn't tell me who he was marrying. I suspect it's someone very famous and intensely publicity-shy. And that's okay. We don't need her input because Brooks was very explicit in what he wanted."

Corinne leaned forward, her expression intense. "So what does he want?"

Teresa half smiled. "He wants me to recreate Delilah Rhodes and Alex Dane's wedding. With one crucial difference…"

Corinne bounced up and down and gestured Teresa to keep talking. "What? What's the difference?"

"Delilah and Alex had a massive budget."

"Our budget is smaller? Dammit. Okay, we can get creative."

Teresa shook her head. "No, we have an unlimited budget. We can spend what we like, how we like, but it's got to be blow-your-socks-off amazing. But we only have two weeks to get everything organized."

Corinne pulled a smile up onto her face in an effort to appreciate the joke. "Ha ha."

"I wish I were joking. But I'm not. Brooks has thrown Limitless Events a lifeline. Minimal time is the cost of that lifeline." Teresa forced a smile of her own. "But, if we work every hour of the day, maybe we'll all still have jobs at the end of the month."

Teresa watched as confusion and disbelief flew across Corinne's face and gave her assistant a minute to take in the news. She'd come into her office thinking that the company could not possibly recover from Saturday night's fiasco but instead of getting pink slips, they were going to organize the wedding of the year.

How did this happen? Why was this happening? Teresa couldn't answer Corinne's questions, not without explaining that she owed someone a favor and that this was his way of collecting. The Fixer had told her, when he checked on Joshua to see if the $7 million debt was real, that she owed him a nonmonetary favor and she was finally being asked to cough up.

She'd always worried that The Fixer would ask her to do something illegal, something below board— she wasn't an idiot; she knew that he wasn't a law-abiding angel—and she was so relieved that he was asking her to use her skills to repay her debt. Yeah, Brooks's time frame was totally ludicrous but, compared to some of the scenarios she'd imagined, this was child's play. And, thank God, legal.

And best of all, Brooks was still going to pay her. Bonus.

Teresa couldn't help wondering how Brooks had heard of The Fixer and whether asking for help on organizing his wedding was all he'd asked of the man who, it was reported, could arrange anything, anywhere. She'd heard of The Fixer through her previous boss, Mariella Santiago-Marshall, but how had Brooks connected with her sure-his-hands-are-dirty angel? It had to be word of mouth, whispered over boardroom tables or over glasses of five-hundred-dollar whiskey. But unlike hers, The Fixer's fee to Brooks was sure to be hard cash.

Hey, she didn't care. She was ridding herself of one debt. And she'd use the enormous fee Brooks had offered her to pay some of Josh's debt, hoping to placate Joshua's money lender and buy them some time.

But nobody would be getting paid if they didn't get to work. Teresa looked at Corinne and issued the first of many instructions. "I'd like you to make up a mood board of all our most expensive weddings to show to Brooks, to get an idea of what he does and doesn't want. Focus on the Newport Bridge wedding."

When Corinne left the room, Teresa stood up and walked over to her window and watched the Seattle-Bremerton ferry cross Elliott Bay. She placed her hand on the window and sighed at the wet, miserable day. Normally, the weather didn't bother her but today it just reminded her of her soggy heart, her tear-soaked soul.

She missed Liam…

Get used to it; you're going to be missing him for a long, long time.

Never again would she feel his mouth on hers, the scratch of his two- or three- or four-day stubble on her skin. Her body wouldn't hum in pleasure as he traced her lips with his, drawing out the anticipation of his tongue moving into her mouth to tangle with hers. She doubted that she'd ever again experience the flood of wet, warm heat between her legs as his hands tightened on her hips and he laid siege to her mouth.

Memories of how he made her feel rushed over Teresa. He'd slowly, too slowly, pull her shirt from the waistband of her trousers or skirt, his fingers drawing bright, bold patterns on her skin. Liam loved to turn her around in order to trace the bumps of her spine, his hard and rigid cock pressing into her butt. No matter how much she begged, Liam treated her like a present he wanted to take his time opening, slowly removing her clothes, one feminine piece at a time. His words burned her skin—"You're so pretty," "God, I want you," "Can't wait to watch you come"— and with a flick of his tongue across a lace-covered nipple, he'd have her hovering on the edge of an orgasm, desperate to take flight.

He'd take his time, too much time, before slipping his fingers into her panties, to find the heat between her slick folds. He always knew how to touch her, whether it was with a flick of his finger or a swipe of his tongue. He'd bring her to orgasm, sometimes once, a couple of times twice, with his fingers and his tongue, not entering her until she was limp and languid and so very, very well loved.

Then he'd push inside her, hot and long and devastatingly masculine and build her up again. And again. And yet again before allowing her to crash and burn and flame.

None of that would happen again.

The thought made her want to cry. But she didn't

because she was Teresa St. Claire, and when had tears helped with anything? No, the best she could do was to soldier on because that was what she did best.

Like brightly colored pieces of a shattered mosaic pile, Teresa always picked up all the pieces she could and rearranged them to make a new pattern or picture. But damn, it was getting harder and harder to do.

In his office at the Abbingdon private airport on the outskirts of Seattle, Brooks lifted his head to watch an ACJ—an Airbus Corporate Jet—land on the runway to the left of his office on the top floor of the office block that housed Abbingdon Airlines' headquarters. The jet was exquisite and the touchdown perfect on the slick runway. Brooks looked at his watch and yep, the limousines were leaving their hangar to pick up the twenty guests who had flown in, as he'd heard, for *Carmen*, playing at the Seattle Opera House. He'd been offered tickets to attend but couldn't remember by whom.

Brooks shrugged. It didn't matter since he didn't have time to waste attending the theater when he had a wife to find, a future to secure.

Pulling his eyes off the ACJ and its fluid, feminine lines, Brooks looked at his computer monitor and opened the email he'd received while he was salivating over the jet. Brooks read the two-word correspondence:

For consideration.

Knowing, without a smidgen of doubt, that the message was from The Fixer, Brooks double-clicked on the first of three files. A photograph of a raven-haired beauty popped up in front of him and Brooks lifted his eyebrows in appreciation. Beneath the photograph The Fixer had a brief paragraph detailing why she was a suitable candidate to become the first Mrs. Brooks Abbingdon. In Mari Ruiz's case, she was a divorcée who'd been skinned by her husband, leaving her with a taste for high living but with no one to fund it. She had two degrees, was a champion ballroom dancer and spoke three languages. She was also a gourmet cook.

Mmm, interesting. Brooks opened the next file, a sultry redhead, who was a young widow looking for a dad for her three kids, all under the age of seven. Brooks dismissed her immediately; this situation was messed up already without adding kids to the chaos. Sighing, Brooks opened the third file and sucked in a surprised breath.

Well, well. Nicolette Ryan wasn't someone he'd expected to find on his computer at nine thirty in the morning. He knew Nicolette, had been introduced to her once or twice and he'd had her microphone pointed in his face on various occasions. She was intelligent and witty and, holy hell, with her long black hair and petite frame, and those expressive, brown-black eyes, as sexy as sin. He liked her. She was the one journalist most of his friends and acquaintances found tolerable.

But why was she on his list of prospective brides? Intrigued, Brooks read The Fixer's report. Nicolette Ryan was, per his comments, brainy and ambitious and wanted to make a break into serious reporting. Apparently, she'd been floating a documentary film to any producer who'd listen but nobody was taking her seriously. The project was important to her—personally important and related to something in her past—and The Fixer was convinced that there was little she wouldn't do to see the project on the big screen.

Brooks scrolled down, annoyed to realize that The Fixer hadn't explained his cryptic comment about her past. Brooks touched the reply button and banged out a quick message asking for an explanation. He was about to hit the Send button when the thought occurred that, had The Fixer wanted him to have that information, he would've given it. A demanding email wouldn't change his mind.

The point was: Nicolette Ryan wanted something and if he could provide her the means to achieve that goal, she might be amenable to a temporary marriage.

Brooks flipped back to look at the picture of the sultry brunette but, compared to Nicolette, she looked over-the-top, too high-maintenance.

He'd met Nicolette; he liked her and there'd been a buzz of attraction when they spoke. It wasn't love at first sight—who believed in that anyway?—but something definitely arced between them.

He was hopeful. After all, everyone had their price—his was Abbingdon Airlines—and he just needed to find out whether her documentary was important enough to her to sacrifice her single status. God, he hoped so.

He was running out of time.

Three

Nobody in Seattle refused to take his calls and Teresa St. Claire wouldn't be the first.

Liam stepped into the large open-plan office and met the wide eyes of the young receptionist sitting behind a sleek desk. Early twenties, first job out of college, wide eyes and desperate to please. Child's play.

"I'm on my way to see Ms. St. Claire."

Liam had to give her credit; she did jump up from her desk and did try to run after him, but his legs were longer and her headphones were connected to her laptop. Besides, he was a foot taller, bigger and broader; how on earth could she stop him?

Walking across the open-plan offices, he ignored the buzz of chatter his presence generated and ignored the eyes boring into his back. Limitless Events occupied one corner of the top floor of this building and high, arched windows flooded the office with natural light. He flicked a glance outside; it was still raining, and he thought that Teresa had a hell of a view. Slowing down, he approached a messy desk in front of the only self-contained office and growled when he saw that the doors were closed. He looked at Teresa's PA, surprised to see her leaning back in her chair, legs crossed, a smirk on her pretty face.

"To what do we owe the honor of your illustrious presence, Mr. Christopher?" Oh, yeah, there was a ton of snark under the sweet smile.

"Cut the crap, Corinne. You know damn well that I've left six messages and that I've been trying to talk to her since early Sunday morning," Liam retorted. "She's avoiding me."

"So you thought the best way to deal with her was to show up at her place of work?" Corinne had the audacity to roll her eyes. "Do you know anything about women, Mr. Christopher?"

Obviously not. Up until Teresa appeared in his life, he thought he had. He could charm them into bed, show them a good time and when he was bored, extracted himself quietly, easing his way out of their lives with flowers or perfume or more expensive gifts, depending on the woman and the situation. Once, when that Russian ballet dancer refused to go quietly, he'd needed to say goodbye with a holiday in Cannes and a diamond tennis bracelet. But generally, women weren't difficult.

And then there was Teresa…

"Can I go in?"

Corinne bared her teeth at him. "Let me see if she has time for you."

Before Corinne could connect the call, Liam turned at the sound of a door opening. Teresa stood in the open doorway, looking beautiful but fragile. Her creamy complexion was two shades paler than usual, her sexy mouth was pulled tight and the bags under her eyes were a darker blue than her irises. But as he was coming to accept, Teresa could look like a ghoul and she'd still manage to turn him on.

"What are you doing here, Liam?"

Since there was only one answer to that question—he wanted to speak to her, dammit!—he shook his head and took two steps in her direction. When he stood close enough to her to inhale her sweet breath, close enough for his chest to flirt with hers, he placed both hands under her elbows and lifted her off her feet. Hell, his woman, *this* woman, needed to eat more! Walking her backward, he deposited her inside her office, back on her two-inch, ice-pick heels—black today to match her severe black suit and, probably, her mood—and kicked the door shut with his foot.

When he heard the snick of the lock, he shoved his hands into the pockets of his suit pants. His hands, stupid things, desperately wanted to pull that black sweater from her skirt and lift it up and over her head. Would her bra be black, too? Her panties? He thought so but he sure as hell would like to make sure.

"I do not appreciate you barging into my office," Teresa told him, trying to sound snotty.

"I do not appreciate you not taking my calls," Liam whipped back, not fazed by her cool eyes and her tight mouth. He knew her well enough to see the pain lurking beneath all that liquid, velvet blue, knew that she was fighting the urge to weep or scream.

She had a right to.

Liam couldn't resist running a thumb over her cheekbone, skirting the edges of her eye sockets. "Have you slept at all since the weekend?"

He knew that her pride had her wanting to lie but at the last minute she shook her head. "No, I've dozed here and there."

"Things will seem better after you've slept."

Teresa stepped away from him and walked away, dropping into the sleek office chair behind her desk. She placed her hands on the table and her amazing eyes flashed blue fire. "So if I sleep, will I wake up and find that my brother didn't gate-crash Matt's party, you didn't hit him, he wasn't seen on YouTube and I didn't have to force him to stay in rehab, with him insisting that he's not an addict? Will that just all go away with some sleep?"

She had him there. "No."

"Exactly." Teresa scratched her forehead and she released a long stream of air and her shoulders fell from somewhere near her ears. "I don't want to fight with you, Liam."

"I don't want to fight, either."

"But I can't deal with you right now. Right now I

have another commission, an event to organize, and everything is riding on it." Teresa picked up a pen and rolled it between her palms. "I can't be distracted and I need to focus. And I really do believe that it's better that we not see each other anymore."

"BS," Liam shot back. "You're just feeling overwhelmed. Possibly scared."

Teresa nodded. "Sure I am. But maybe I am also trying to protect you. I'm not good for you, Liam."

Liam slapped his hands on his hips, anger coursing through him. She sounded too much like his mother, who'd made her own disparaging comments about Teresa over the past few weeks. Not good enough, a tart, so little class. They were both wrong but there was only one person whose mind he wanted to change. "I'm a big boy. I don't need you protecting me."

"No matter what I say, there are people out there, including your mother, who believe I had an affair with your father, who think I've only latched on to you because I have my eyes on your company."

He didn't give a rat's ass what other people thought and, honestly, he didn't care much what his mother thought. "So? Let them think what they want."

A pencil hit his chest and dropped to the floor. Liam looked at it, raised one eyebrow and returned his eyes to Teresa's face. On the plus side, she had color in her cheeks. She also looked like she was about to blow.

"Liam, *listen* to me. You and me, it's… Whatever the hell we had, it's over! Whatever it was, it's done."

Liam sent her a steady look. "I'm not trying to be a jerk, Teresa, but it's not as easy as that."

"Just go, Liam. Please."

God, this woman was as stubborn as a boulder. He could tell her that their attraction hadn't died, that it would take more than her calling it to end this craziness between them. They couldn't just switch off the taps and walk away. Like her, he couldn't define what they had but it sure as hell wasn't something that could be simply and easily dismissed. He'd tried that several times and it never worked. But that argument wouldn't work with her so he latched on to what was tangible. "Linus's will stipulates that we still have to work together at Christopher Corporation for a whole year."

His statement detonated fireworks in her eyes. And not the good kind. "The corporation? That's what you are thinking about?"

Well, no. He was thinking about taking her to bed but knew that if he made that suggestion he might leave her office minus a few of his essential body parts.

And that thought pissed him off, big-time. And once he acknowledged his anger, it took on a life of its own. He'd been worrying about her for days and he had to storm her citadel to check whether she was okay.

Teresa placed her fingertips on her forehead. "We can't keep doing this, Liam. At some point we have to accept that we are bad for each other."

Liam surged to his feet, walked over to her chair

and placing his hands on her waist, pulled her up. He gripped her luscious butt and yanked her into him, allowing his hard erection to push into her stomach. "Feel that? That isn't bad, dammit!"

Teresa looked up at him and he could see her body warring with her brain, each equally stubborn. He dipped his head down and slapped his lips against hers. Her mouth immediately opened beneath his and he swept inside, determined to show her that desire like this was worth fighting for, holding on to, keeping. Yeah, they weren't great at communicating but this, this they could do. This they couldn't fake, lie about, deny.

As for the other stuff, they could work on it…

Liam felt Teresa soften and when she pressed her breasts into his chest, he slowed his kiss down, needing to savor her, to explore her intense combination of flavors. He could taste her hazelnut-flavor coffee, toothpaste and a tart sweetness that was all Teresa. Pulling her jersey up, he placed his hands on her lower back, easily spanning her slim waist. The smell of soft, fragrant, heated skin drifted up to his and he felt his knees soften, his head swim. This was the only woman who'd ever managed to create fog in his brain, remove the saliva from his mouth, shut down his thought processes.

Not for the first time Liam decided that she scared the crap out of him.

Liam pulled back from the kiss and lifted his hand to hold the back of her head, his fingers pushing up and under the loose bun she habitually wore. Risking her ire but needing to see her hair down, he pulled out her pins and her thick blond hair cascaded over his hands, down her back. With her hair down she looked softer, more vulnerable and younger and, if that were at all possible, sexier.

Teresa rested her cheek on his pec and lightly placed her hands on his waist as if she couldn't decide whether to hold him or not. "Stop fighting me, Teresa, and let me hold you."

Teresa stiffened in his arms and then he heard her long sigh and slowly, so slowly, her arms moved around his body and she buried her nose in his shirt.

"Everything is so messed up, Liam."

And she was, as she always did, trying to handle everything herself. "I know, honey."

"I can't let you help. I don't know how to accept help," Teresa said, her voice so low he had to bend his head to hear her soft words. "I need to sort this out myself, Liam."

He dropped a kiss into her hair. "Why?"

Teresa took her time answering. "Because people have told me, all my life, that they would be there for me. Then they left."

"I won't do that to you, Teresa."

Teresa pulled back, pulled her teeth between her lips and when Liam looked into her eyes, the pain within them nearly dropped him to his knees. "Maybe, maybe not. But I can't take that chance because you, disappointing me again, is a step too far, a bridge that will blow up once I cross it. I'm not strong enough to cope with that, as well as the rest of my life falling apart. Frankly, Liam, I'm starting to believe that I'm not very strong at all."

Teresa walked over to her desk, stared down at it and tapped her finger on the sleek wood. He watched her profile as her eyes moved from her desk to the window to right at the view of Elliott Bay. When she spoke again, he heard her uncertainty and, dammit, the fear in her voice. "I need some time, Liam, probably quite a bit of it."

"I can't give that to you," Liam replied.

Christopher Corporation, and the terms of his father's will, demanded her presence and involvement in the company. And besides, if he gave her the space she demanded, wouldn't he be doing exactly what she expected, running when she needed him to plant his feet and stick?

"My brother owes money to dangerous people. Money that I am in the process of trying to find. I have a high-society, over-the-top wedding to organize in two weeks' time so that I can save my company's reputation and buy us some time with those previously mentioned mobsters. And I still need to face Matt Richmond and apologize once again for ruining his gala evening."

"While organizing a wedding isn't in my skill set, I am thrilled you have work and I know you will do a fantastic job. I will bring you late-night pizzas and early-morning coffee if that's what you need me to do." She was listening to him so he took the opportunity to float a few options available.

"Allow me to lend you the money to pay off your

brother's debts. I have the money and we can work out a repayment plan because I know that you are too proud to take a handout. Yeah, apologizing to Matt is something I can't do for you but I can hold your hand while you do it."

Teresa closed her eyes and Liam desperately wanted to rub away the single tear that dared to escape. But he knew that if he acknowledged her emotion, he'd lose her. So he just kept his eyes on her face and waited for her response.

"Please go, Liam. Go before I take you up on one or all of your sweet offers. Go before I start to believe in you."

To hell with that. Instead of walking to the door, Liam wrapped his arms around her and held on tight. Resting his chin in her hair, he held her until he felt her body stiffen, until she started to push away. Knowing he'd pushed her far enough today, he decided to retreat so he placed a kiss on her temple and released his grip. "I'm going to go. But I'll call you later, okay?"

Teresa nodded.

Liam tipped her chin up with the side of his thumb and waited until her eyes met his. All that deep, velvety blue was a sharp smack to his heart. "And when I do, take my damn calls."

Four

Teresa watched her office door close behind Liam's rather fine back view—oh, who was she kidding, viewed from every angle Liam was sexy—and she staggered to her chair and dropped into it, feeling like a leaky balloon. She could fight with Liam, roll around the sheets with Liam but Liam being kind, sensitive? Generous? She hated him acting like that.

But only because you want to curl up in his arms, in his strength. You hate it because it tempts you to take a breath, to allow someone else to take the wheel, to steer the ship. And God forbid that you let go for one minute. Who knows what could happen? The world might stop turning!

Teresa frowned at her inner sarcastic self and picked up a pen, thinking that it was high time she went back to work, that she paid some attention to saving her business.

But as hard as she tried, she couldn't concentrate.

Was she that much of a control freak? Possibly. Handing over control to anyone on anything made her feel twitchy and disoriented. Yes, she kept a tight control on her life, and her emotions, because if she didn't, people side-winded her because she made the mistake of trusting them to do what they said they would. Her father had told her, time and again, that he'd always be there for her, that he'd never leave her, that she was "his girl," but when he needed to make a choice, he'd left the country and never returned. She shouldn't be angry at him for dying but, dammit, she was.

Her mother was also skilled at making promises she couldn't keep. "I'll get a job next week, honey."

"Yes, I promise I'll come to your school recital."

"I will stop drinking, smoking, staying out late."

Words, to her mom, were cheap, and promises weren't ever something that were meant to be kept. To her taking the easy way out was always the better option and that words were easily forgotten. Joshua followed in their mother's footsteps but Teresa went in the opposite direction.

Because words spoken did have consequences, and promises were supposed to be kept. She refused to cut corners and she never made excuses. And she owned her life, her choices and her mistakes. But maybe because her childhood and teenage years had been such a tumultuous time, maybe she did now try to control every little thing so that it wouldn't come back to bite her in the butt.

So yeah, she owned that she was a control freak and wasn't able to roll with the punches. But punches hurt, dammit, and why should she have to experience the pain if she could avoid it altogether?

Teresa heard the brisk knock on her door and then Corinne pushed it open. "Hey, you have an unexpected visitor."

Corinne's emphasis on *unexpected* made Teresa sit up straighter. "Who?"

"Me."

Oh, hell, no! Teresa watched as Nicolette Ryan brushed past Corinne to stand just inside her office. Teresa looked past Nicolette to Corinne, who lifted her hands in a "what-could-I-do?" shrug.

So far this morning, both Liam and this entertainment reporter had pushed by her gatekeepers and barged into her office. If this was going to be a trend, she'd need better security.

Teresa narrowed her eyes at Corinne before transferring her gaze onto the petite woman standing in front of her. She was gorgeous; she'd always thought so. With her black hair hitting her waist and brown-black eyes, even features and a spray of freckles across her nose, Nicolette was a combination of vamp and girl-next-door and, as a result, had millions of fans of both sexes. She wore a tight, deep navy skirt and a white, long-sleeved, plain silk shirt that skimmed her curves and the most amazing, quirky pair of bright red heels.

Teresa, reluctantly, felt herself tumbling head over heels in love with her shoes.

"I do like your style."

Teresa winced, wishing she could pull the words back. She was supremely annoyed with this woman—her ongoing coverage of Saturday night's suck-fest had kept Matt's disastrous gala in the news—and she didn't want to admire a damn thing about her.

But to be fair, she liked Nicolette's dress sense. She always managed to look classy despite wearing tight and short dresses and sky-high heels. Yeah, she showed a bit of cleavage and a lot of leg but she never stepped over the line into trashy. And the same could be said of her reporting; she never made sly innuendos or flirted with the truth. She reported on what she was told and didn't embellish.

And maybe that was the only reason Teresa hadn't tossed her through her partially open window to the street below.

"You have a lot of cheek showing your face here," Teresa stated, pleased with her calm voice.

"It's been said that the one attribute I don't lack is cheek." Nicolette gestured to the seat on the opposite side of her desk. "Do you mind if I sit down?"

"If you've come to ask me for a follow-up interview, then I really wouldn't bother. I don't have anything to say."

Nicolette sat down, crossed her legs and swung her foot. "I'd love you to give me a comment, or better, an interview—"

Teresa growled and Nicolette grinned. She held

up her hand. "As I was about to say, that's not the reason I'm here."

Teresa didn't believe that for a minute but okay, she'd hear her out. "Then why don't you get to the point and tell me why you are here?"

Nicolette inhaled and Teresa noticed the panic in her eyes and her tight grip on her handbag. "I'm getting married and you, apparently, are planning my wedding."

No, she wasn't. Teresa knew that it had been a tough couple of days but she was pretty sure that she'd never agreed to organize Nicolette Ryan's wedding.

The girl was crackers, possibly delusional. "Okay, so who are you marrying?"

"Brooks Abbingdon."

Yeah, it still didn't make any sense.

And Teresa St. Claire looked as gobsmacked as she still felt. Because, really, Nic was still waiting for a camera crew to pop out from behind a door or a screen, yelling "just kidding" and "you've been pranked."

Nic turned her head to look at the closed door to Teresa's office but it wasn't opening; she could hear no movement behind the door. Nobody, dammit, was there and nobody was about to return her life to normal, to tell her that this was a big mistake, a dream, a crazy prank.

"You are marrying Brooks?" Teresa said after another minute of stunned silence.

Nic nodded.

"Okay, wow." Teresa stood up, placed her hands on her desk and pulled in a deep breath. "I didn't know that you and Brooks were seeing each other."

They hadn't been. In fact, up until yesterday evening, she'd just admired—okay, lusted and drooled over—Brooks from afar. His visit to her apartment last night changed everything. No, his proposal had upended her life and sent it spinning in a whole new direction.

And it was one she needed to take.

"Take every opportunity to tell Jane's story, Nic. Promise me."

"I promise, Gran."

Did that promise cover marriage? Surely not. But a big and bright opportunity came with the marriage and that was covered by her promise to her dying grandmother ten years before. So there was no, or very little, wiggle room. And Brooks had been clear; marriage meant funding for her project, guaranteed distribution and the opportunity to make a difference. If she didn't marry Brooks, her project—the one that was dear to her heart and the one she spent every spare minute she had working on—would never see the light of day. And she couldn't let Janie, or her grandmother, down.

Teresa stood up straight, shook her head and looked bemused. "I don't know what to say. And when I find myself without words, coffee normally works. Would you like some?"

Nic thanked her and Teresa left the room, muttering something about it being a helluva day. Nic dropped her bag to the floor, uncrossed her legs and stared at the old, original hardwood floor. She couldn't believe that she was sitting here, in Teresa's office, talking about her upcoming wedding to one of Seattle's most eligible bachelors.

A man she thought sexier than Idris Elba and hotter than Charlie Hunnam. A man who'd, for some odd reason, wanted to marry her. In a couple of weeks' time.

Was this really happening to her? She hadn't dreamed everything that happened last night?

It had been a normal Tuesday evening and she'd been in her apartment, working on Jane's project, something she did whenever she had a free moment. She'd also been waiting for a pizza delivery and muttered "Hallelujah" when her intercom buzzed. Thinking it was her regular pizza man, she told Pete to come on up, hitting the button to open the front door downstairs. Knowing that Pete ran up the stairs, she waited a minute before heading to the door, flinging it open. God, she was hungry…

Instead of a classic margherita pie, Brooks Abbingdon stood in the hallway, his fist raised.

"You're not my pizza." But damn, she could've taken a bite out of him as easily.

Brooks's grin was slow, sexy and machine-gun lethal. "Sorry to disappoint you."

Instinctively, she knew that she couldn't give this man an inch or he'd take her a thousand miles. And she might let him. *Get yourself and, more important, your hormones under control!*

"You should be sorry because I'm starving and while you smell good, my pizza smells better."

Brooks's mouth twitched with amusement and those eyes, an unusual shade of gold, lightened. "Care to share?"

Nic deliberately attempted to look and sound bored. Difficult when her stomach was doing loops under her rib cage. "Care to tell me why you are standing outside my door?"

"Share your pizza and I will."

He might have a story he wanted covered, a piece of hot gossip. While most of her sources called her on her private number or emailed her, one or two had asked to meet her face-to-face. Though none had, admittedly, had the balls to show up at her door.

Should she take a chance and let him in? Or should she insist that they meet in a public place? What the hell could Brooks Abbingdon want to tell her? She'd never once thought he was the type to dish dirt.

But why else would he be here?

Nic quickly recalled what she knew of Brooks Abbingdon, immediately discounting his wealth and good looks. All his ex-girlfriends, and they'd been a few, had only good things to say about him…he was a nice guy, a gentleman, that he'd make a great husband if he ever chose to settle down. Because he treated his exes well, Nic thought she'd be safe enough if she let him into her apartment.

"My sharing my pizza depends on why you are here." Nic stepped back into her hallway and jerked her head to tell him to come inside. She closed the door behind him and sent him a cool smile.

By the time she'd put a beer in his hand and invited him to sit, her pizza had arrived and Nic, above Brooks's objection, handed Pete his money and carried the box back into the living room. She placed the box on the coffee table in front of Brooks and walked into her kitchen to choose plates and silverware. It annoyed her to realize that she'd chosen her best plates and had dug two linen napkins out of a drawer. Was she really trying to impress Brooks?

Irritated, Nic dumped plates next to the box and handed Brooks a napkin. She opened the box, slid a piece of pizza onto her plate and tucked her feet up under her bottom. Brooks surprised her by picking up a slice of pizza and putting the pointy end straight into his mouth. He swirled a piece of melted cheese around his finger, sucked it off and Nic felt a wave of hot heat surge between her legs.

Do not jump him, do not stand up and slap your mouth against his.

"Good pie," Brooks said in between bites. "Where do you order from?"

"A little Italian place on the next corner," Nic replied. Because she hated feeling so out-of-control attracted to him, she put a whole bunch of spice into her voice. "I thought the deal was that you tell me something good and *then* you share my pizza."

Brooks rested his arms on his muscled thighs, his hands dangling between his knees. Then he looked her dead in the eye and when he spoke his voice was heart-attack serious.

"Okay, if you insist. I want you to marry me. In two weeks' time. If you say yes, I will provide you the funding to produce your documentary project and I will open doors to you so that it can get the widest distribution possible. I have enough money and connections to make sure that happens."

Nic laughed at his absurd statement and rolled her eyes. She was about to tell him to stop wasting her time and then his words sank in. He knew about her project…

He knew.

About her project.

Nobody, apart from a handful of people she'd spoken to about Jane's Nightmare, knew how she spent her free time. How on earth had Brooks found out?

"How do you know about my documentary?"

Brooks waved her words away. "I just do. And it can happen, if you marry me."

Honestly, this was too bizarre, like a scene out of a B-grade movie. Who shows up on a Tuesday evening and starts proposing to a random woman? And, despite their meeting once or twice before and some very mild flirting, she was very random indeed.

"This is a good opportunity for you, Nicolette."

Yeah, first time she'd heard marriage described in those terms. Nic tipped her head. "Okay, I'll play your ridiculous game. What if I say no?"

Remorse flickered across his face but it was quickly chased away by determination. "Then I kill your project. I have enough money and contacts in the entertainment world to do that, as well. And by kill it, I mean it will never see the light of day. *Ever.*"

Brooks reached for another slice of pizza but Nic was quicker. She whipped up the box and pulled it onto her lap. She stared at Brooks, wondering if behind all that sexy was insanity. "Are you mad? You're talking crazy, and crazy talk does not get rewarded with pizza!"

Brooks simply pulled the box from her, helped himself to another piece of pizza and, in between bites, explained his offer. They'd be married in name only, for a period of time yet to be determined, but the marriage had to, to keep the gossip to the minimum, last longer than a year.

In addition to funding her documentary, she'd also get a significant amount of money for one year as his wife. For every additional year they remained married, she would receive a large sum of cash. If, after a year, she wanted out, he wouldn't contest the divorce.

Children weren't a prerequisite but he wasn't opposed to fathering a child. Should she choose to have one with him, he'd pay her living expenses, post-divorce, for the rest of her life. But that meant them sleeping together and while she wished she could emphatically state that would only happen when hell iced over, honesty had her admitting that she'd have difficulty avoiding his bed.

Really, what hot-blooded—or even moderately warm-blooded woman, wouldn't? He was hot. As in blistering.

"Why do you need to get married?"

"You don't need to know that."

"And why do you need to be married by month's end?"

"You don't need to know that, either." Brooks's reply left her with more questions than answers. He'd given her until this morning to decide—a scant eight hours!—and she'd spent all of last night pacing her apartment, both intrigued and pissed that she was considering saying yes to his ridiculous offer.

Oh, she didn't care about the money and, while she did want kids sometime in the future, she didn't need to marry to get one. So the only reason to consider Brooks's offer was related to how important it was for her to tell Jane's story and to highlight human trafficking. She owed it to her sister. She needed to tell the world about her because maybe, just maybe, it would save one girl's life.

She worked with street girls, spoke to at-risk teenagers, but her documentary would reach so many more people, might save more lives. And, on screen, Jane would always be remembered.

When Brooks called her at half past seven this morning, she'd agreed to his crazy proposal. The man, damn him, hadn't seemed surprised to hear her reluctant "yes."

It was almost as if he knew her better than she knew herself.

Nic heard footsteps behind her and watched as Teresa placed a tray on her desk, the smell of freshly ground beans wafting her way. Since last night she hadn't been able to eat or drink and her tongue started to salivate. It took all her willpower not to grab that mug of coffee and suck it down.

Teresa leaned her butt against the edge of the desk and crossed her feet at her ankles. Cradling her cup in her hands, she looked at Nic over the rim. "I'm not very happy with you right now."

Honestly, she had bigger worries than gaining Teresa St. Claire's approval. "Because of my coverage of Matt's party? Or my reporting on the ensuing chaos?"

"The latter." Teresa lifted one slim shoulder. "Wouldn't you be?"

She wouldn't lie. "Sure. But any journalist worth his or her salt would've covered the story."

Teresa started to argue, hauled in her words and Nic's Spidey sense quivered. She slowly lowered her cup her mouth and looked at Teresa. Why was she acting squirrelly?

"You organized Matt's event. You didn't have anything to do with that guy crashing the party," Nic stated and saw Teresa's eyes flare at the mention of the young man. "Nobody could blame you for the bad ending."

"Of course they can't," Teresa quickly replied. Too quickly. Why did she think Teresa was lying? Oh, hell, yes, there was much, much more to this story than she was privy to. And, while she wanted to push and pry, to get to the heart of the matter, she couldn't because she wasn't here as a reporter, she was here as Brooks Abbingdon's fiancée.

And how bizarre did that sound? But maybe she could be both…

Before she could formulate her first probing question, Teresa pulled up a big smile that was as fake as the plastic surgery she routinely saw on the red carpet. "So you're going to marry Brooks."

Apparently so.

"That's so exciting! How long have you been seeing each other?"

Nic wished she could tell her that they'd met fourteen hours before but knew that would be placing a match to a flame of gas. "Long enough."

Long enough to decide to sacrifice her freedom for her career and for a project she'd promised her gran she'd complete.

"Brooks told me that he wants an over-the-top, blow-your-socks-off wedding. He's given me an unlimited budget and no instructions except to tell me that it will happen in two weeks' time, venue to be decided."

Nic pulled in her breath, shook her head and nailed Teresa with a hard glare. "That's not going to happen. It will be a small, understated wedding with minimal fuss, preferably in court."

"Okay," Teresa muttered. "Flowers?"

This was a business arrangement not a parade. "None."

"Do you have a dress?"

"I have a white pantsuit that would be suitable," Nic lobbed back.

Teresa looked like she'd swallowed a bug. "Guests?"

"Him, me and whoever is authorized to marry us," Nic said, her tone final. "Do we need anyone else?"

Leaning back, Teresa picked up her phone and tapped the screen with fast-moving fingers. Nic heard phone ringing and realized that Teresa had put the phone on speaker mode. Brooks's deep "Hello" sent a shiver of awareness down her spine. She was stupidly, ruthlessly attracted to her wretched blackmailer!

"Brooks, we have a problem," Teresa calmly stated.

"I'm paying you an extraordinary amount of money for there not to be problems, Teresa," Brooks stated.

"Well, I have no problem spending your money but your fiancée definitely does. You both seem to have very different ideas on what you want from this wedding and I am, not surprisingly, confused."

"Is she there with you?" Brooks demanded.

Nic answered before Teresa could. "*She* is. And *she* is not happy about any of this."

He was a smart man; he'd understand that she was talking about more than the wedding. "You've made that clear, Nic."

Nic? Nobody but Jess and Gran called her Nic. Coming from his mouth her name sounded feminine and, dammit, sweet. Almost tender.

"What I suggest," Teresa said in her no-nonsense voice, "is that you two meet and decide what you want. Bearing in mind that I have minimal time, I need you to get back to me by tomorrow morning on exactly what type of wedding you want. And I need you to cover everything: flowers, music, guests, type of food, potential venues, budget. *Everything.*"

"What a nightmare," Nic muttered. She was still getting used to the idea of getting hitched; now she had to make definitive decisions around her wedding day? Could she take a breath first?

"All right," Brooks agreed. "We'll meet up tonight and thrash it out."

"Good. I need everything you come up with by tomorrow morning," Teresa said, her tone crisp. "And Brooks?"

"Yeah?"

Teresa smiled at Nic and Nic sensed a warming of her polar-cold attitude. "If you want people to take this engagement seriously, you should buy your fiancée a ring. Preferably one that can be seen from space."

Five

Later that day Teresa, shaky with hunger and exhaustion, heard the sound of a heavy masculine tread outside her office door and barely had any energy to react. If the person outside her door was a burglar, he could take what he wanted. If it was someone with nastier ideas, well, then, she didn't much care. She was *that* tired.

But really, logically, it was probably just Dan, the night janitor, waging the war on dust bunnies and trash baskets.

Pushing her glasses up onto her nose, Teresa stared at the figures on her Excel spreadsheet, trying to make sense of the data on the screen. She'd been crunching numbers all afternoon, building cash flow forecasts and up-to-date financials. She needed accurate information regarding her company, boiled down to how much she had (x) and that would last her how long (y)?

Without Brooks's commission, she was looking at weeks, not months. With his project she had another six months. But what happened after that? Would she have work? Would her reputation recover? Had it taken too many hits?

What then? What the hell would she do?

Teresa placed a hand on her stomach, felt the room spin so she turned sideways and dropped her head between her knees. For the first time since she was a kid she felt truly scared, utterly vulnerable. She couldn't lose her company, it was what she did, who she was. This was all she had.

And she hadn't even addressed the issue of sucking money from the company to make a part payment toward Joshua's debt.

Teresa felt the energy in the room change and one of the many ropes wrapped around her lungs loosened. When Liam placed a large hand on her back, another rope dropped away and she felt like she could suck in a tiny breath.

Damn him for making her feel better, stronger, more in control. "Take a long, deep breath and try to relax."

Teresa wanted to lift her head to send him a "get real" look but her head felt like it weighed the equivalent of a baby elephant. And if she could relax, she wouldn't have her head between her legs and the room wouldn't be spinning. But her dizziness might also be a result of not eating for the last forty-eight hours. Coffee didn't have the nutritional value of vegetables or protein. Frankly, coffee really needed to up its game.

When Teresa felt like her lungs could function, she lifted her head and was happy to find that the world had stabilized. Liam, wearing faded jeans and a cranberry-colored sweater, was on his haunches in front of her, looking all handsome and hot. She leaned forward to kiss him but he just placed the back of his hand against her forehead.

"You don't have a fever. Do you have a stomach-ache?"

Teresa swatted his hand away. "Stop fussing, Liam. I'm fine. What are you doing here?"

Liam placed his forearm on his knee, innately at ease as he rested on the balls of his feet. "You are not fine. You are exhausted, hungry and stressed out. Overworked and at the end of your rope."

Teresa rolled her eyes, uncomfortable with exactly how accurate his diagnosis was. "I needed to run some figures."

"At nine at night?" Liam retorted. He stood up and placed his hands on his hips. "It couldn't wait until tomorrow?"

Probably. But she would not have been able to sleep until she had an accurate view of where she stood. Then again, she probably wouldn't sleep now that she did have an accurate view of the situation. Facing bankruptcy was an excellent reason to stay awake worrying.

Teresa leaned back in her chair, raising her head to look into Liam's frustrated face. "Why are you here?"

Liam picked up her phone and waved it from side to side. "You're not answering your phone. Again."

Teresa snatched it out of his hand and tapped the screen. When it remained stubbornly black, she grimaced. "It doesn't have any juice."

"Which is an accurate description of you."

Liam bent over, rested his hands on her knees and Teresa felt lust, and warmth, dance across her skin. "We need to talk about the next Christopher Corporation board meeting and your expected attendance."

Teresa opened her mouth to argue but Liam squeezed her knee. "But not tonight, honey. Tonight all you need to do is eat and then sleep."

Throw a bath and sex into that scenario and she would be in heaven. Actually, maybe just a bath because, as talented as Liam was and however much she craved his touch, she simply didn't have the energy for anything more.

Liam stood up, took her hands and pulled her to her feet. Teresa looked at her monitor and hesitated. She had a few more scenarios to run, figures to input. "It'll still be there in the morning."

She should stay here. Teresa tugged her hand from Liam's and shook her head. "I think I should stay."

"Well, that's not going to happen," Liam said, picking up her dead phone. He tucked it into the back pocket of his jeans. Teresa accepted that her reactions were super-slow because, before she could figure out what he was doing, her tote bag was over his shoulder and her car keys were clutched in his fist. He gestured to the door. "After you."

Not happening. Liam Christopher had no right to barge into her office and order her around. Who did he think he was? Who did he think he was dealing with? Some weak-willed female whose knees would buckle at his display of dominance? Okay, her knees were a bit jelly-like but that had more to do with lack of food than his caveman approach to an argument.

"Do you really think your bossy attitude is going to work with me?"

Liam had the cheek to grin at her. He shook his head. "Not at all. But I am stronger and bigger and this will." He bent his knees, placed his arm under her thigh and another around her back and Teresa found herself cradled against his broad chest.

By the time her shock receded enough for her to speak, they were inside the elevator and heading to the basement parking garage. And when the elevator doors opened, she was yawning and thinking that this position wasn't too uncomfortable, and conceding that she neither had the energy to protest his high-handed tactics or his bossiness. Really, this was the second time he'd used his physical strength on her and she should protest…

She *would* protest. Sometime soon.

But the leather seats of his expensive car were heated and comfortable and if she turned her head and pulled her knees up, she could pretend she was in her bed…

Brooks had seen Nicolette in tiny lamé dresses, rocking three-inch heels and in short skirts and tight tops, so to discover that she was just as sexy in loose-fitting yoga pants and an old T-shirt came as a shock. Her face was also makeup free and she looked a lot younger than her twenty-eight years.

Brooks ran a finger around the open collar of his shirt and wondered if he was making a mistake, not sure if Nicolette was the right person for this crazy venture. Barefoot, her long hair pulled up into a pony-tail, she looked softer, vulnerable and nothing like the sophisticated reporter he'd encountered a few times before.

"Are you going to stand in my doorway or are you going to come inside?" Nicolette demanded.

Brooks stepped into the hallway of her apartment and shrugged off his jacket, relieved to hear the acer-bity in Nicolette's tone. Acerbity he could handle.

"Good evening, Nicolette," he said, hanging his jacket on a coat hook.

"For goodness' sake, call me Nic." Nic waved him to the couch. A pair of glasses stood on the coffee table, as well as a bottle of red wine. He picked up the wine and examined the label, surprised to see it was from a small winery in South Africa. He might be mistaken but he thought he might have toured the winery when he visited that country a few years back. He picked up the bottle and poured wine into two glasses and, before taking his seat, handed a glass to Nic. "Take a seat."

Nic narrowed her eyes at his bossiness but curled up into a single chair, tucking her bare feet under her luscious ass. She sipped her wine before resting the glass against her forehead.

"Tough day?" The words slipped out before Brooks could pull them back. It was a stupid question; he was blackmailing her into marrying him. How could she be having a good day?

Nic, thank God, chose not to respond. "So let's talk about this farcical arrangement we are entering."

Okay, then, straight to business. "Absolutely, since Teresa needs some answers."

"So do I," Nic replied. "I know why I am sacrificing my freedom and my single status but why are you doing this? What's prompting you to marry a woman you don't even know? Are you gay?"

Brooks grinned, not at all offended. Some of his favorite people were gay. "Nope."

His eyes dropped to her cleavage, to the soft skin on display, and lust shot straight to his groin. He was very not-gay. He started to swell and didn't really care if she noticed. The sooner she got used to the idea that he was intensely attracted to her, the sooner he could take her to bed. And, judging by the way her cheeks flushed at his blatantly sexual stare, she'd had a sexy thought, or two, about him.

Good, one less mountain to climb.

"Just like you, I need to marry to reach a goal."

"What goal? What are you trying to achieve? You didn't tell me anything last night," Nic demanded, and Brooks could see why she was such a good reporter. The woman was tenacious.

What harm could it do if he told her? He didn't

think she would turn his words into an article but, just to cover his bases, he tossed out the question, "Off the record?"

Nic's sour expression conveyed her annoyance at his question. When he didn't speak again, she lifted her hands in frustration. "Of course it's off the record. I'm not going to write a story about my fiancé!"

She had the reputation of playing it straight, of not repeating stories told to her in confidence, so Brooks allowed himself to relax a fraction. "In order to access a lot of cash from Abbingdon Trust, I need to be married. And I need to marry either on or before the last day of the month, which is my birthday."

"I thought that you are wealthy. What do you need money for?"

Yeah, her curiosity wasn't easily satiated.

"I own a forty-nine-percent share in Abbingdon Airlines," Brooks explained. "The remainder of the shares are owned by my grandfather, in his personal capacity, and he wants to sell his stake. If I am married on my thirty-fifth birthday, I inherit a load of cash via the Abbingdon Trust and I can buy complete control of Abbingdon Airlines."

"Are you certain your grandfather will sell to you and only you?"

Brooks knew that his smile was a little self-satisfied but he was still proud of himself for inserting clauses into his agreements with his grandfather that provided for such an eventuality.

"As per our agreement, he has to sell me shares if and when I have the cash. I would've been happy for him to keep the shares if he wasn't dead-set on using his shares as collateral on another silly, guaranteed-to-lose-his-shirt business proposition."

Nic took a healthy sip of her wine. "What would happen to the cash if you weren't married by thirty-five? Would you lose it?"

Brooks shook his head. "Nope. Every five years the offer is made, with the same conditions."

"So why didn't you get married at thirty?" Nic asked.

"Didn't need the money, hadn't met anyone I wanted to marry, there was no urgency to." Brooks shrugged. "Now there is."

"And I'm the sacrificial goat."

Brooks felt a spurt of annoyance and the acid taste in the back of his throat. Was he that bad a catch? Was this really the worst thing that could happen to her? He had all his teeth and hair, wasn't a complete jerk and intended to keep her in a style any woman could easily become accustomed to. He was going to fund her documentary, introduce her to influential people who'd make sure her film received the exposure it needed.

And when they parted, he'd inject a significant amount of cash into her bank account. Why was *she* acting like she was headed toward the hangman's noose?

And why did he care? Why did her approval matter so much? Generally, he didn't care what people thought about him but Nic's approval, for some insane reason, seemed to matter to him.

Nic put her wineglass down on the coffee table

and lifted her arms to tighten the tie holding her long, thick hair off her face. Her breasts lifted and Brooks sucked in his breath as he saw the freckles on her chest, a hint of her lacy white bra. God, anyone would think that he hadn't had a woman in years instead of weeks...

But he'd never had Nic.

And why that should make a difference he had no damn idea.

"Let's talk weddings," Nic said, her tone brisk and her eyes cool. "Why the big push for something wildly over-the-top?"

"It's an opportunity to throw a helluva party on someone else's dime." Brooks placed his ankle on his opposite knee. "And also because it will generate publicity. For me, for Abbingdon Airlines and for you."

Nic frowned. "For me?"

"Sure. You're an entertainment reporter and your marriage to me will generate a lot of interest and grow your profile exponentially. That will help you generate publicity when you start publicizing your documentary. You want as many people to see your documentary as possible and the higher your profile, the more that will happen."

Nic reached for the bottle of wine and dashed some liquid into her empty glass. "You haven't asked me about my documentary or inquired why it's so important to me."

Brooks had thought about it, had wanted to commission a deep background check on her but stopped himself. For some strange and probably asinine reason, he wanted Nic to tell him herself, to open up to him when she felt comfortable to do so.

"When you want to, you'll tell me without coercion."

He wanted to get to know this woman who was going to become his wife. She fascinated him on levels he found disturbing.

And if he had a choice, he'd probably run as far as he could from her, and this marriage. She made him think about what it would be like to marry, to have a smart and gorgeous woman as his life partner.

And now he felt like he had a noose around his neck.

Teresa, feeling renewed after nine hours of sleep, walked into the open-plan living area dressed in an old boyfriend's T-shirt. Stepping into her living room, she glanced out her living room window and looked down the street to the narrow view of Elliott Bay. The sun was out, the sky was blue and she swore that, if she opened her window, she'd hear birds chirping.

It was amazing how much a beautiful day and nine hours of solid sleep could improve her mood.

And, yeah, seeing Liam Christopher leaning against her kitchen counter, shirtless and with the top two buttons of his jeans open, revealing his sexy happy trail, was guaranteed to lift her mood even higher. Unnoticed by him, she leaned against the wall and waited for him to finish his call, perfectly happy to spend a couple of minutes checking him out.

Messy hair, a three-day growth on his cheeks and

chin and easing down his thick, strong neck. The muscles in his broad shoulders were well-defined and flowed into sexy biceps that were big and, well, bitable. A light dusting of black hair covered his upper chest and a fine trail of hair bisected his six-pack, another part of his body she loved to nibble. Teresa pouted at the jeans covering his long legs but she easily remembered the muscles in his thighs, his strong calves and yep, she even liked his bare feet.

And that was the problem: she wasn't only half in love with Liam Christopher—she *liked* him. Love would be easier to ignore if she wasn't as attracted to his personality and his brain as she was to his body. God, why couldn't they have met at a different time, been different people? What if she had just bumped into him at a coffee shop and they dated like normal people? Why did Linus have to leave her shares in Christopher Corporation? Why did their pasts have to be so damn complicated?

"I need you to dig as deeply into the past as you can. Don't be scared to turn over rocks."

It took a minute for Liam's words to sink in and she frowned. Who was he talking to and why would he need anyone to investigate his past? What was going on here? Peeling herself off the wall, Teresa continued walking to the kitchen and watched as he turned his head to observe her approach. His green eyes darted over her face, down her body, and her nipples puckered in response to his appreciative look. His eyes hovered on her breasts before sliding down her thighs and over her bare feet.

"Oh, and can you suggest a reputable lab who can do genetic testing? I'm prepared to pay a premium for some rushed results."

Curiouser and curiouser.

Liam ended his call and tossed his phone onto the kitchen table and then gripped the counter behind him. The action made his stomach ripple and his biceps flex. It also sent heat to her core and she felt the slow burn between her legs. Oh, God. How was she supposed to resist him looking so sexy, and a little sad?

"Everything okay?" Teresa asked. She desperately wanted coffee but her coffee machine was behind Liam and if she came within a foot of him, she'd start begging him to do her on the floor.

You are not going back to that make love, fight, break up circle again. Enough now.

"Yes, no. Sort of."

Well, that was as clear as mud. Before Teresa could push him to explain, he spoke again. "You look much better this morning. You slept like the dead."

"And how would you know that?"

Liam's smile could heat up the sun. "Within two minutes of leaving your office you were out for the count. So I brought you here. I carried you from the car to your bed and you never woke up once." His grin turned naughty. "And, God, you weigh a ton."

Since her doctor kept telling her that she could do with picking up a pound or two, Teresa didn't react to his teasing. She just lifted her brows and tried to look haughty.

"I undressed you, put you to bed and, after showering, crawled in after you."

"You could've gone home," Teresa pointed out.

Liam lifted one shoulder in an easy shrug. "I was tired and I like your place. I always have."

Teresa looked around her light-filled condo and nodded. She liked her place, too. It was filled with natural colors, comfy furniture and luscious plants. She could relax here, be herself. There weren't many places she felt comfortable enough to shed her cool-as-a-cucumber persona, and this apartment, and her office, when she was alone, were probably the only two in existence. And Liam was the only person who'd ever seen her emotionally naked.

And that made her feel vulnerable. And weak. And scared.

And because she was feeling off-kilter, she lifted her nose in the air and put ice into her voice. "You do remember that I broke up with you, don't you? That I told you I didn't want to have anything to do with you, that we were unfixable?"

"I do. But I'm ignoring you."

Teresa's mouth dropped open at his insouciant reply. How dare he dismiss her feelings? And that reminded her. How dare he pick her up and lug her around like she was a bag of cement? "You can't just ignore me and we need to address your caveman antics, as well."

Liam sent her a get-real look.

"Seriously, Liam, this isn't going to work. You and I, we don't work. We make love, we think we might have a chance and—" Teresa made her hands explode, mimicking a bomb detonation "—*boom*! It all blows up. We try again, another explosion. We don't talk, we don't trust. I think life is trying to tell us that we aren't supposed to be together."

Liam surprised her by nodding his agreement. "Maybe. But I'm thinking that it might be telling us to slow down, to take it easy."

"What are you talking about?"

"It's just been problem after problem with us, drama after drama. Maybe if we were better friends we wouldn't be very volatile. Everything wouldn't be such a production. We'd stick around instead of bolting." Liam rubbed the back of his neck. "Because that's our default reaction when things fall apart. We try and put distance between us and the problem."

"And you don't trust me."

"I don't trust anyone, Teresa. But I'm going to work on that," Liam said, his voice somber. "And you have to accept that there are some things that can't be fixed according to your timetable. Or at all."

Because a part of her still believed that her father didn't fight hard enough to get back to his family when his visa expired, Teresa knew that she tended to go overboard in pushing for what she wanted. She simply never wanted to live with regrets, with "what if I'd done that" thoughts. And yes, because she couldn't go back and understand her father's inability to come home, and his subsequent death, she did try to fix situations and people.

But trying to fix her and Liam was a lost cause. Even she knew that.

Didn't she?

"We bolt, Teresa, when things don't go our way or turn out the way we want them to. It's a fault we both share."

They'd both been scarred by their pasts and it was second nature to protect themselves. And they both recognized that the other had the power to hurt, to scald and to scour. But how would being friends help, and how on earth would they manage to ignore the passion that always flared between them? They could barely be in the same room without wanting to attack zippers and buttons.

God, she couldn't have this conversation without coffee. Teresa walked over to the counter to stand next to him, pushing him to the side with a nudge from her shoulder. Her bare arm brushed the skin of his and heat flashed. Goose bumps also danced on her skin.

Teresa threw up her hands in frustration. "That! That's the problem right there! You touch me and I want to fall into your arms and kiss you stupid."

Teresa dropped her eyes to his crotch and she noticed his erection starting to swell, straining the fabric of his jeans. "And look! It's not just me."

Liam groaned and rubbed his hands over his face. "I will admit, it's…inconvenient!"

"It's uncontrollable." Teresa placed both her hands on his shoulder and pushed him to the edge of the counter. "Stand over there! And put a damn shirt on!"

"Bossy," Liam muttered, a small smile touching his lips.

"You're only figuring this out now?"

Teresa turned her attention back to the coffee machine and darted a look at Liam's back as he walked across her living room to the hallway and then, she presumed, to her bedroom where he'd left his shirt and shoes. He was gone but a minute and Teresa wished it were five, or ten. She needed to wrangle her libido, to get blood to her brain. Damn Liam Christopher for having this effect on her.

Teresa watched coffee drip into her mug and considered putting her mouth to the spout to get some caffeine into her system. Hearing Liam's footsteps, she turned around and he was fully dressed, thank God. But only looking slightly less sexy. She still wanted to jump him.

"You can go now," Teresa told him, waving toward her front door.

"Yeah, that's not going to happen," Liam said, walking over to her and filching her cup of coffee from under the spout.

Teresa stared at him, thoughts of stabbing him between the eyes with a rusty fork dancing across her brain. "Do you want to die?"

Liam sipped before handing her cup back to her. Teresa placed her lips where his had been and thought that she could taste him. She was losing it, it was official. Not bothering to add milk or sugar, she pulled out a chair and dropped into it as Liam reached for another mug on the shelf above her machine and tapped the side of his fist against the start button.

"Let's go back to what we were discussing."

Teresa groaned. "Let's not."

Liam glanced at his half-full cup under the spout before picking up hers and taking another sip. Teresa growled but didn't have the energy to argue. She was saving her strength for bigger battles. She could not allow Liam to persuade her to try again, to be drawn back into his life and his orbit. Yeah, the highs were fantastic but the lows had the ability to drop her to her knees. She'd walked away from him in Napa Valley and she needed to keep on walking.

They were bad for each other...why wasn't he seeing this?

"Just go, Liam."

Instead of listening, Liam dropped into a chair and tapped his fingers against his coffee mug. "I want to apologize for not telling you that I hired an investigator to look into your life. He's still digging and has been, for several weeks. I ordered him to find everything and anything."

Teresa immediately noticed that he was apologizing for not telling her, not apologizing for hiring the detective. "I told you that I would tell you anything you needed to know about me!"

"The thing is... I don't think you know what I need to know."

Say what? It was still too early to have such a convoluted conversation. Liam's eyes darkened. "I can't move on. I can't go forward until I know why Linus left you those shares."

This again! "For the millionth time, I did not sleep with your father!"

Liam held up his hand. "I know that, *I do*. But there has to be a reason why he left you the shares worth millions. I want to know what that reason is because I'm tired of living in darkness, constantly wondering and waiting for information. I'm done with it. I want to pull all the skeletons, dirty or not, out of the cupboard and damn well deal with them!"

Teresa stared at him and saw the determination to find the truth in his eyes. Not sure what this meant, for him or them, she remained quiet.

"I feel like we are trying to build something, you and I, on shaky ground. We need all the facts about everything."

"I told you about Joshua, about the debt that he owes," Teresa responded. Didn't he realize what a huge step that was for her?

"And I appreciate you doing that," Liam said and after some thought, spoke again. "According to my guy, Joshua's debt was sold on to an outfit in Vegas. This new group specializes in hard-to-recover debt. They are, according to his sources, looking for Joshua and there's no doubt that they now know he's back on the West Coast."

Liam tapped his finger against his coffee cup. "Did you ask your brother why he gate-crashed that party?"

Of course she had. "He said that he was in a bar back east and he vaguely remembers some girl offering to buy him a drink. That's when his memory goes fuzzy.

"He remembers thinking that I was in trouble and the only way to save me was to go to the Goblet and confront my enemies. That's what he was trying to do by standing up and making a fool of himself."

"So he got drunk on the East Coast and six to eight hours later he still hadn't sobered up?" Liam asked, skeptical.

Teresa hadn't had a proper conversation with Josh in weeks and she had no idea about his mental state. Should she tell Liam about the puncture wound on his arm?

Before she could decide, Liam leaned forward, his expression intense. "He was drunk on the East Coast, so drunk that he couldn't remember what he did or said, but he bought himself a ticket, got himself on a plane and still made his way to Napa Valley and found you? And if he did manage to do all that while pissed, don't you think he might've sobered up at one point and wondered what the hell he was doing?"

She'd had this thought a few days back but she'd dismissed her suspicions. "He had help," she stated.

Teresa told Liam about the injection mark on his arm and he frowned. "Well, I think that confirms our working theory that he had help."

"But why would somebody track him down, liquor him up and escort him across the country to ruin an event you were organizing?"

Panic closed her throat and Liam immediately reached for her wrist, his thumb tracing patterns on her skin. Teresa immediately felt her vocal cords loosening, air flowing into her lungs.

"Breathe, honey," Liam ordered her, his voice soft. But his eyes and expression were anything but tender. "Somebody has it in for you."

"Or maybe for Matt Richmond?"

Liam shook his head. "Then why use Joshua? No, honey, this is all about you. Maybe it's the loan shark trying to force you to cough up but I don't think so."

"Why not?"

"Because they don't play around by ruining events. No, they are more likely to cut off little fingers or break a kneecap to get someone to pay. Trust me, they'd go straight for the jugular."

She was sorry she'd asked. Teresa felt her stomach lurch. "Oh, God."

"There's no doubt about it. You need to pay that debt, Teresa. As soon as possible."

"When he called me, telling me about the debt, a part of me thought that it was a mistake, like the kidnapping was a mistake."

"They are being deadly serious, Teresa."

"I don't have the money…" Teresa saw the offer on his lips and his next sentence confirmed her assumption.

"I can loan you the money. It'll take me a day or two to get it together but I have it, Teresa."

She was so conflicted, her pride and her protective instincts at war. She couldn't risk Joshua getting hurt, not when Liam was providing her with a reasonable alternative. Since she'd be selling her Christopher

Corporation shares to him at the end of the year, it would be a temporary loan.

Borrowing money from Liam made sense. Dammit. But…not yet. "Thank you for the offer…"

"But?"

Teresa shook her head. "No buts, well, maybe a small one. I am just going to wait until they contact me again, making demands for the money. I don't know how to get in touch with them and they told me not to try. When they do, *if* they do, I'll ask you for the loan."

Relief made Liam's eyes greener. "When they make contact again, you need to tell them that you want proof that, if the debt is paid, no one else will come after you later. They need to give you a guarantee."

Teresa nodded, feeling lighter. "Thank you. I owe you. Joshua owes you."

Liam smiled and his eyes dropped to her mouth, and Teresa knew that he was no longer thinking about money and debts and lenders. He leaned forward, his mouth so close to hers that she could smell his sweet, minty breath, count the individual hairs in his scruffy beard, see the small scar on his bottom lip. She wanted him to kiss her, to take her to bed and away from thoughts of debt and mobsters and inheritances she didn't want. She wanted him to take her to bed where there was only his touch and his taste and the way he made her feel.

Teresa lifted her hand and rubbed her thumb

against his bottom lip, surprised at how soft his lips were. Was he ever going to kiss her?

Liam gently pulled the tip of her thumb between his teeth and bit down. Teresa sucked in her breath at the spark of pleasure-pain and sighed when Liam gently sucked her digit. How could she be so turned on by him kissing her thumb?

"Teresa?" Liam whispered.

"Mmm?"

"Can we try and be friends? Can we also try to work together to get to the bottom of why Linus left you shares?"

Liam's teeth scraped the side of her thumb and she shivered. "Mmm-hmm."

"Oh, so I'll expect to see you at the Christopher Corporation shareholders meeting the day after tomorrow? I should also have the seven million ready for you by then."

"Okay."

Teresa heard her response and something about it sounded wrong. Wait, what had he said? She pulled back and stared at him while rewinding the conversation in her head. Her mouth dropped open, then closed and then opened again.

"You're catching flies." Liam leaned back, folded his arms and smirked. Teresa wanted to smack him sideways.

"You were trying to seduce me to get your own way!" Teresa accused. "That's a crappy thing to do! That's not playing fair."

Liam laughed. "Honey, nobody ever said life was

going to be fair." Standing up, he dropped a hard, openmouthed kiss on her lips. When he pulled back, he smiled at her and Teresa felt her stomach, and her liver and her kidneys, do backflips. "But damn, it can be fun. Later."

Liam walked out of the kitchen toward her front door and Teresa tried to think of something cutting to say. The "I hate you" she tossed in his direction fell well short of the mark.

At the door, Liam turned and smiled again, causing her poor organs to take flight once more. "No, you don't."

No, she didn't. Not even close.

Six

Liam lied.

The board meeting was as horrible as she'd thought it would be. As Liam guided her out of Christopher Corporation's ultra-modern boardroom, Teresa glanced back into the room to check that the blond hardwood floors weren't, actually, blood-stained.

Because it felt like she and Liam had been drained of a pint or two.

Teresa glanced up at Liam's hard face and grimaced at the anger she saw blazing from his eyes, the tension tightening his jaw and the frustration thinning his mouth. How he'd held his temper, kept so even and calm, while his father's contemporaries attacked him from all sides, Teresa had no idea. He'd remained calm when their ire was directed at him but when one of the members turned his vitriol on her, Teresa saw the first crack in his seemingly impenetrable armor. As long as she lived, she'd never forget his cold, hard words spoken in defense of her.

"You can criticize me, criticize my leadership and my work ethic and my decisions but Ms. St. Claire is off-limits. Am I clear?"

Teresa shivered at his ice-cold, CIA-interrogator voice and she'd watched, reluctantly fascinated, as the board members leaned back as if to avoid the wave of Liam's ire. When nobody made a counter comment, Teresa knew that she could, fractionally, relax.

And she tried to, she did, but then one of the members passed a motion suggesting that Liam be removed as CEO. Teresa knew that Liam didn't expect the meeting to go well but that was a rocket he hadn't expected to be launched, nor detonated. She was seriously impressed by his self-control.

Teresa watched as he simply smiled, leaned back in his chair and loosened the button of his immaculately tailored suit jacket. He tapped the point of his capped pen on the surface of the sleek table and locked eyes with his opponent. Liam's quiet words, his sensible response, knocked that rocket right out of the sky.

"Ladies and gentlemen, we are all getting ahead of ourselves. Yes, it's been a rough couple of months. Yes, things have happened that haven't placed the company in the best light but I have a contract and you cannot fire me without cause. And if you do, I will sue the pants off you and, trust me, that will not be in the company's best interest.

"Now, may I suggest that we all take a deep breath and start thinking instead of reacting emotionally?"

"Your father wanted you to be CEO, Liam. Not all of us agreed with that," the chairman of the board pointed out.

"Noted. But according to company policy, I am entitled to some time to prove myself," Liam replied, looking unfazed and even bored. Teresa, furious for him, sat on her hands and clenched her teeth in an effort not to defend him. He wouldn't appreciate it and she respected him enough to allow him to fight his own battles. This was, after all, his arena.

"And we will be watching you. And may I suggest that you distance yourself from Ms. St. Claire, Liam?"

Liam's face hardened further and Teresa saw his fist clench. "You're out of line, Bosworth."

"I am protecting this company."

"Christopher Corporation is my responsibility, mine to protect."

Bosworth smiled and gestured to the rest of the board members. "Actually, with this new distribution of shares, it's all of ours to protect, look after, to steer. And should Ms. St. Claire decide to divest her shares to someone other than you, this situation will become very interesting indeed."

Like that would happen. She had no idea why Linus left her his shares but she'd never consider selling them to anyone but Liam. They were his. Did he know that? With all the other craziness happening around them, had she even explained that to him? Could he be in doubt of where her loyalties lay?

Teresa raised her hand to speak and Bosworth gave her a condescending smile. "I think we've wasted enough time on this subject. Moving on to item six…"

"But—" Teresa protested.

"Moving on, Ms. St. Claire."

She'd been dismissed and disrespected and Teresa had to exert a substantial amount of self-control not to demand to be heard. Besides, it didn't matter what the board thought, as long as Liam knew that she would never sell her shares to anyone but him. That was all that was important.

But jeez, she wouldn't mind educating Bosworth and his cronies about equality and fairness.

Teresa felt Liam's hand on her back as he guided her down the long hallway to his executive office in the corner of the building. When they reached his office, Duncan, his PA, jumped to his feet, his expression worried.

Liam stopped by his assistant's desk and the two men exchanged a long look. "Was it as bad as you thought?" Duncan asked.

"Worse."

Duncan ran his hand over his mouth before defiance sparked in his eyes. "Screw 'em. What do we need to do?"

Liam's mouth finally kicked up at the corners in the tiniest of smiles. "They are a necessary evil."

Duncan folded his arms and rocked on his heels. "They," he stated, looking annoyed, "are a bunch of rickety old geezers who should've been put out to pasture decades ago."

Teresa grinned. She really, really liked Liam's young PA.

Liam briefly clasped the younger man's shoulder before opening the door to his massive office and gesturing her inside. "Coffee would be good. It might help me maintain my 'haven't killed anyone yet' streak."

Liam closed the office door behind him and Teresa, rested his forehead on the door and banged his head against the wood, releasing colorful combinations of curses. In his own office, away from prying eyes, he could release his iron-tight grip of control and allow the rolling waves of anger to consume him.

Folding his arms above his head and resting his forearms on the door, Liam closed his eyes and tried to make sense of the past two hours. Oh, he knew that the board wouldn't be happy about the recent events. He and Christopher Corporation had received some negative publicity but he genuinely believed that the dip in share price was mostly due to current economic conditions and nothing to do with his leadership or Teresa or the shares. But the board members were using it as an excuse to oust him, to put someone else behind his desk. Why?

Why didn't they want him running the company his father created?

Because, unlike his father, he wasn't a negotiator; neither was he easily swayed. He did things his way, set a course, and the board either came along for the ride or was left on the sidelines. He wasn't a yes-man and he wanted autonomy. His father ran the board like a democracy; he had no intention of allowing a bunch of, mostly, doddery old fools charting the course of his modern, technologically rich company. They feared what they couldn't understand and Liam wanted to take the company into places and markets they didn't understand and couldn't relate to.

They were scared, and scared men did stupid things. Like firing him from his own company.

But Jesus, they'd crossed a very big line when they attacked Teresa. Yeah, he had a million unanswered questions about her but she knew that she'd never do anything to harm him or Christopher Corporation. Despite everything she'd been through, she'd held her head high and marched on through the flames. Today she'd been polite and brave and kept her dignity while those around them lost theirs. She was an asset to the corporation and, yeah, to him.

He couldn't let her go, wouldn't let her go. When he'd first seen her seven years ago, sitting across the family dining table, he'd instinctively recognized that she was important to him, to his happiness.

He'd known her, recognized her. He wanted to claim her, to make her his. He wasn't that young man who saw everything in black-and-white anymore; he knew that life was a lot of gray. But his possessiveness toward Teresa remained as strong as it always had been.

And he was damned if he'd allow anything else to happen to her. From this day on, she was under his protection. And protect her, he would.

Liam pulled away from the door and walked over to

his desk that sat at right angles to the floor-to-ceiling windows. If he looked south, he could see, on clear days, Mt. Rainier; north, the iconic Space Needle and west, West Puget Sound. If he looked east, the view was of his door and Teresa, staring at him with big, round eyes.

With her hair pulled backed into a loose bun and dressed in a tight black skirt and a tailored, open-neck white shirt she looked every inch the corporate drone. But if one looked at her feet and noticed her tangerine heels, that impression of a tightly wound, composed woman was blown out of the water.

But really, he just had to look into her expressive blue eyes to see what she was thinking. Her eyes reflected every emotion lodged in her soul and yep, confusion and concern reigned.

"Would you like to explain what just happened in there?"

Teresa was a bright woman; she knew he'd just been put on notice. She was really asking whether he had a plan. He didn't need one; his position was safe for at least six months and by then, he would've completed a few deals and seen some projects come online, like the joint Sasha Project with Richmond Industries. The share price would be up and those fickle bastards would be satisfied. He wasn't worried about the company; he was worried about Teresa.

Her company was in dire straits; she needed to secure her brother's safety; she looked like she was on the edge of falling apart. Except that she wouldn't because she was too damn strong to do that.

She needed someone to stand in her corner, to show her that she wasn't alone, to be there for her.

That could all be easily accomplished if she married him.

Liam swallowed, tried to push the thoughts of being married away but couldn't dislodge the thought. As his wife, Teresa would be quickly accepted by the highest echelons of Seattle society. That acceptance would translate into business for Limitless Events and his business associates would also funnel their events her way.

If she married him, he'd have a reason to immediately pay off her brother's debts—he'd tell her that he couldn't afford for anyone to discover that his brother-in-law owed mobsters money. Quickly settling her debt would ensure her safety and that was intensely important to him.

And if they married, she wouldn't be alone anymore.

Was he in savior-complex mode? Liam heard Matt's question in his head and pulled his eyes off Teresa to look out his window. Matt often accused him of wanting to save everyone and everything because that was what his mother demanded of him, and his father, growing up. Linus had refused to rush to her rescue, to pay attention to her every want and need, so Liam provided her with the attention she craved.

Matt was convinced that he was conditioned to wanting to help if someone was in crisis. It was, his best friend told him, his biggest weakness and his most powerful strength. Matt also frequently told him that his savior complex would come back to bite him on the ass.

So be it. Teresa needed help and he was going to give it to her. But how best to do that? Was marriage the only answer?

"Take a seat," Liam told her, gesturing to his sleek white couch she was standing behind.

Teresa sat down and tucked one orange heel behind the opposite calf. She was so very graceful, every movement fluid. He just wanted to take her to bed. Hell, a bed wasn't even necessary; he could lock the door and make love to her in the late-morning light, stripping her naked as the world went on outside without them.

A sharp knock on the door and Duncan walking into the room dissolved that fantasy. Duncan placed a tray holding a carafe of coffee, cups and cream and sugar on the coffee table in front of Teresa and lifted his eyebrows at Liam. After a beat, Duncan nodded briskly. "Enjoy your coffee. I'll make sure that you aren't disturbed."

Liam squirmed, thinking that the younger man might be able to read his mind. When Duncan left the room, he took his seat opposite Teresa, linked his hands and waited until her eyes met his. There was one way to get her under his wing, to put a message out there that she was off-limits, that she was under his protection.

"I think we should get married. As soon as possible."

Teresa thought she heard Liam asking her to marry him. Which wasn't possible. *Was it?*

Before she could force her tongue to form words—not that she had the vaguest idea of what she should say, apart from "are you nuts?"—Liam stood up and loomed over her, one hand on the arm of the sofa, the other behind her head, caging her in. She stared into his beautiful eyes, fringed with those dark, thick lashes, and lifted her fingers to the scruff on his square jaw.

She'd go back to harsh reality in a minute—a freakin' marriage proposal?—she just needed to touch him, inhale his sexy scent, lose herself in his forest-green eyes.

Teresa watched as his mouth descend toward hers and she pushed away the thought that they should be talking about business, that she needed to respond to his crazy suggestion. She didn't want to be sensible or businesslike or strategic; she just needed to feel.

Kissing Liam, touching his wonderful, masculine body, made sense; nothing else did.

Confusion and lust warred for dominance in Liam's eyes. "I shouldn't be kissing you—" he said.

Screw that.

"The only thing you should be doing right now is kissing me." Teresa whispered the words against his lips.

Liam released a harsh swear before his mouth covered hers and as his tongue swept into her mouth, Teresa, for the first time in days, relaxed. Here, in Liam's arms, was where she felt safe, protected, totally at ease.

Teresa wound her arms around Liam's neck and stumbled to her feet, needing to be closer to him, wanting, if possible, to crawl inside his skin and stay there. She pushed her breasts into his hard chest, mentally cursing the fabric barriers between them.

As Liam's hand moved from her head, over her back and down her ass, Teresa gripped the fabric of his shirt at his hips and pulled it out from the waistband of his suit pants. Pushing her hands up and under the fabric, she finally found hot, male skin covering long, sleek muscles. Heat and need and warmth soaked her panties as she pushed his shirt up his chest, wrenching her mouth away from his to place hot kisses on his right pec, flicking her tongue across his flat nipple.

Above her head, Liam cursed and she felt his hands pulling at his tie and undoing the top button of his shirt. Then he lifted his shirt up and over his head and she had easy access to his wide chest and ridged stomach.

"You're so hot and it's been so long and I want you so much," Teresa told him as she dropped her hands to his belt buckle and pulled it apart, her fingers struggling to undo the clasp of his suit pants.

If she didn't get him inside her, filling her and all those empty, bleak places, she might just cry…

"Hold on a sec," Liam muttered.

Teresa ignored him and when he pushed her hands away, using one hand to loosely clasp her wrists behind her back, he used his other hand to tip her chin up. His eyes met hers and his sweet smile liquefied her knees. "Slow down a sec, honey. I need to get you caught up."

Teresa stared at him as he dropped his hand to flick open the buttons of her silk shirt and when he spread the fabric apart and stared down at her barely there bra, passion flashed, hot and bright, in his eyes. "You are so beautiful."

In that moment, watching Liam as he looked at her, Teresa felt beautiful. Thoughts of marriage and mergers and machinations fell away and she knew that he wanted her. Liam's long finger traced her breasts above midnight-colored lace and when his thumb drifted over her nipple, she sucked in her breath and wobbled on her heels.

Liam released her hands, hoisted her skirt up her hips and spun around, dropping to sit on the sofa behind him. Her skirt, now up around her hips, was no longer a barrier to movement so he spread her knees across his thighs and positioned her so that her hot core was directly positioned over his rock-hard erection. Teresa felt her eyes cross and her breathing became shallower as she rocked against him.

It wouldn't take much for her to come…

Pleasure spiked when Liam pulled the cup of her bra down and sucked her into his mouth, his tongue winding around her tight nipple. Teresa held the back of his head and whimpered, the hurricane of pleasure whirling and swirling around and within her.

Liam pulled away from her and looked up, his eyes slamming into hers. "This is truth, Teresa. This is the only truth. The way you make me feel…this is where truth lies."

Unable to take in his words, to discern what he was

trying to say, Teresa arched her back, only concerned that he give her other breast the same attention. When he did, she ground down on his cock, needing to feel him, every hard inch of him.

"Tell me you want me," Liam muttered, pushing his hand between them to pull down his zipper, his knuckles brushing against her clit. Teresa gasped, demanding more.

Between her legs, Liam's hand stilled. "Tell me."

Teresa forced her eyes open. "I want you, Liam." She pushed against his hand. "Can't you tell?"

Liam kept his eyes on hers as he lifted his hips, pulling his suit pants and his underwear down his hips. Teresa sighed when she felt his heat and hardness, stroking her core up and down his long, lovely length.

Liam did a half sit-up and reached for the clasp of her bra, flicking it open. He pulled it off and, still arched, bent down to suckle one breast, then the other.

Teresa pushed her hand between them and gripped his cock, moving so that his tip was positioned at her entrance, delaying the pleasure of feeling him slide into her for as long as possible.

"Condom, Teresa."

She couldn't wait and what was the point? "I'm on the pill."

Relief flashed across Liam's face and, two seconds later, he lifted his hips and surged into her in one hard, soul-touching stroke. Teresa sighed, sank deeper onto him and wrapped her arms around his shoulders, conscious of his face in her neck, his breath against her skin. This was a curiously intimate position. She wasn't sure who was cradling whom but it didn't matter… Liam was inside her, where she needed him to be.

"You feel amazing," Liam muttered, rocking his hips with small movements and sending bursts of pleasure coursing through her. But she needed more; she needed everything. She needed hard and long and intense…she needed *him*.

This.

Teresa pulled back, held his face in her hands and met his foggy-with-pleasure eyes. "I need you, Liam. I need hard and hot and long and rough. I need you to make me forget everything but how you make me feel."

Liam dropped another curse. "I'm holding on with everything I have, honey. If I take you hard, I'm not going to last a minute."

"I'll be with you every step along the way," Teresa assured him.

He looked at her for a moment, silently questioning her, and something in her face must've convinced him because he surged to his feet, easily picking her up. Ignoring the pants around his hips, he put her on her feet and turned her back to him and placed a hand between her shoulder blades, forcing her to bend over the arm of the sofa. He stepped out of one trouser leg and used his knee to nudge her legs apart. His hands kneaded the bare flesh of her ass, and Teresa heard the snap of the thin cords of her thong breaking and, out of the corner of her eye, saw the dark blue fabric flutter to the floor.

Liam crowded her, his erection resting between her butt cheeks as his hand traveled across her flat stomach and his fingers brushed the thin strip of hair. Expertly, knowingly, his fingers found her clit and Teresa gasped and instinctively lifted her ass. Taking her massive hint, Liam slid into her from behind and Teresa placed her forearms on the sofa arm and buried her face into the crook of her arm.

"No, I need you close," Liam muttered, wrapping his arm diagonally across her chest and pulling her into him, her back to his front. His other arm wrapped around her waist and she felt his mouth on her shoulder, in the crook of her neck.

Needing more, Teresa turned her head and his mouth met hers, his tongue echoing the smooth slides of his cock as he pushed into her and pulled back.

Pleasure, hot and white, shot with silver and white, started at her toes and sprinted up her calves, her thighs, and lodged itself in her womb. It grew brighter and bigger and bolder and when Liam pulled back and placed his hands on her hips and slammed into her, that ball of brilliance shattered and a million sparks danced across her skin. Liam groaned and shuddered, his forehead on her spine.

Teresa closed her eyes, wanting to hold on to the dream for as long as possible. But when Liam kissed her shoulder blade, when he pulled out of her, she knew that reality, and her life, was about to smack her in the face again.

Liam bent down and picked up his suit pants and her bra and shirt. As she took her clothes from him,

Teresa flushed when she realized that her skirt was still up around her hips and her heels were still on her feet.

"My private bathroom is through there," Liam said, his voice low as she held her garments with a shaking hand. "And when you come back, we can discuss getting married."

Teresa stared at herself in the mirror above the sink and shook her head. Judging by her foggy eyes and her swollen mouth, it was obvious to see that she'd just been thoroughly ravished.

Ravished...

It was such an old-fashioned word but it really captured the essence of the moment.

Teresa gripped the edges of the basin and stared down at the white porcelain. As wonderful as making love with Liam was, she had to concentrate. Liam wanted them to get married...

She'd rather stab herself between the eyebrows with a rusty fork.

Oh, she couldn't imagine spending her life with anyone but him, but she was damned if she'd use marriage, even marriage to Liam Christopher, as a business solution, as a logical solution to a sticky situation!

Who did that?

Apparently, good-looking billionaires who wanted to save their jobs and their company. While she didn't want Liam to get ousted as CEO of Christopher Corporation—he was the company and it needed him, no matter what those dinosaurs said earlier—she wouldn't sacrifice herself to the cause. She respected herself too much to settle for less than true love and can't-live-without-you. And she needed trust.

He didn't believe in her. And he still didn't trust her.

And, to be honest, did she fully trust him? Could she ever fully trust anyone again, to trust that he'd stick by her through thick and thin, sickness and health, all that richer and poorer stuff? She didn't know, she didn't think so…people simply didn't do that anymore but she more than wanted that sort of commitment. Having grown up without any support system, she *needed* it.

And then her thoughts started to spiral. Why did he want to marry her, why now? What was driving him? Liam wanting to marry her might also be an easy way for him to get his hands on her shares… without paying for them.

And if he did that then she wouldn't have a way to bulletproof her business and, more important, to pay Joshua's debts so that he would forever be free of those cretins in Vegas.

There were a million reasons why she couldn't marry Liam but at the heart of it was the fact that he didn't love her, didn't trust her and never would. She was already mostly miserable without being married to him; getting the legal system involved would make her feel a hundred times worse.

Through the thick wooden door Teresa heard him clearing his throat. "Teresa, we need to talk."

She really didn't want to. She'd far prefer it if she could walk out of the bathroom and keep moving until she left his office, his building, Seattle and her life. Until she reached the white sands of Bali…

Teresa opened the door and slowly walked back to his sofa, trying not to remember how amazing she felt not ten minutes before. She picked her tote bag up from the floor and slung it over her shoulder. She looked at him, now fully dressed, his tie loosely slung around his neck and his hair messy from her fingers. For a minute he didn't look like the calm and always-in-control Liam Christopher she knew and fought with. He looked like a man waiting on a woman's answer, uncertain and a little worried.

A small part of her wanted to say yes, to give him the answer he needed. Then she remembered that he didn't love her and he didn't trust her or believe anything she said.

No, as great as the sex was—and it was fan-freaking-tastic—she couldn't give him the answer he wanted. She wanted love. Was that too much to ask for?

"No, Liam."

It took a moment for her words to make sense and when they did, shock passed across his face and lodged in his eyes. "What?"

He'd heard her; he just didn't want to accept what she'd said. "No, I won't marry you."

Not for a business. Her self-respect, her happiness, her soul, wasn't for sale.

Seven

Nicolette flashed a smile at Brooks's driver as he opened the back door to his limousine. She slid inside and surreptitiously pinched herself. Taking her seat, she looked past Brooks's broad shoulders as he followed her inside the vehicle and caught a glimpse of the elegant, discreet sign to the left of the red door. Paul's was, if not the best restaurant in Seattle, within the top three. Sitting down for a meal in the twelve-seater restaurant was more difficult than booking a flight to space, but when Brooks asked her where she wanted to eat, she'd tossed out the name of the restaurant as a joke. He'd made it happen.

Brooks. Made. Stuff. Happen.

Brooks settled in beside her, looking utterly masculine in a charcoal suit and an open-neck, white button-down shirt. She looked at his big hand resting on his thigh and wished that it was on her leg, that he was turning to face her, about to lean in for a kiss. Nic swallowed once, then twice. She really, really wanted to kiss Brooks, had from the first moment they met.

How was she going to live with him, in his house, share his life and not jump him on a regular-to-often basis? She was a red-blooded woman in her late twenties and she liked sex; she *needed* sex. And she desperately wanted to get naked with her soon-to-be husband.

Nic sighed and flicked the diamond-and-emerald engagement ring Brooks placed on her finger earlier that evening. It was ridiculously big and stupidly expensive and she couldn't help wishing that the ring came with a heartfelt "I adore you" or "I'm so glad that you are mine."

Gah!

The limo pulled away and Nic turned her head to stare out the window, annoyed at the burning sensation in her eyes.

This is a business arrangement. Why are you allowing yourself to feel all gooey? Stop it right now.

She had to remember why she was doing this, what she was trying to achieve. If she could save one girl...

"My sister and I were close as kids but when she hit her teens, things started to go wrong."

She felt Brooks's eyes on her, could feel his gaze tracing her features. She didn't need to see his face to know that his entire focus was on her. She needed to tell him why her documentary was important, *imperative*, partly so that he would understand why she'd agreed to marry him and also to keep her feet firmly on the ground. This wasn't about love, it wasn't about money…she was doing this to tell Jane's story.

Nic felt Brooks's hand on her thigh, his touch comforting and not sexual, and she sucked in a deep breath. She could trust this man with her secrets; she was sure she could.

"My older sister and I were raised by my grand-mother. My mom…" God, how could she say this?

Brooks squeezed her bare thigh in silent support. Nic forced the words through her teeth. "My mom liked booze a little too much and men even more."

"Your dad?"

Nic lifted one shoulder. "Jane and I had different fathers. She met hers once, I think. Mine was long gone before I was born."

Brooks lifted his hand from her thigh and pushed his hand between the seat and her back, sliding his arm around her waist. He pulled her into him so that her back was against his chest, her head against his shoulder. She felt him kiss her hair, so softly, so… kindly.

Kindness was, she decided, so very underrated.

"Jane, like my mom, liked alcohol and men. She started using both when she was about fourteen. My grandmother put her into rehab a few times but it never took."

Behind her, Brooks tensed but then his hand came up to stroke her hair, his silent support tangible. "At sixteen she met a guy, someone a lot older, and she ran away from home to be with him."

"Oh, honey."

"When I was eighteen and she twenty, we were informed that she'd died of a drug overdose. The investigator from the Medical Examiner's office told us that she'd been working the streets to feed her addictions. When I asked about the guy she ran away with, she told us that Jane lived with her pimp and, by his description, I knew it was the same guy she left with years before."

"Why didn't she make contact?"

It was a fair question. "Embarrassment? Fear of rejection? Coming home would also mean failure and she would've known that Gran and I would've made her face her demons."

Brooks ran his fingers up and down her arm and his light touch gave her the strength to carry on with her explanation. "The investigator handed over her personal effects and there wasn't much. A few clothes, a couple of photos of us as children and an expensive smartphone she'd hidden under a floorboard. I was surprised to see the phone because I thought she would've sold it for crack but she didn't. I went through the phone and on it were twenty, thirty videos, some long, some not."

Tension rippled through Brooks and she turned abruptly, immediately realizing that he'd jumped to the wrong conclusion. Facing him, she linked her fingers in his, needing the connection. "No, they weren't sex videos. It was, I suppose, a diary of sorts. She told her story, her struggle with drugs and addiction, why she ran away. She detailed how her boyfriend and pimp forced her to have sex with multiple men for money in different hotels daily. And that she did it because she felt she owed him, that without him she was nothing. That she, in a warped way, loved him.

"It's a story that plays out a thousand different ways for a hundred thousand girls daily in America, millions across the world. Trafficking doesn't always mean sex rings and forced captivity. Sometimes, most times, it can be just one girl, one guy. And drugs and prostitution and trafficking go together like a hand in a glove."

"And that's why you want to do the documentary," Brooks said, tucking a strand of hair behind her ears.

"That's why *Janie* wanted me to do the documentary. She knew that I was studying journalism and she made the videos for me, hoping that I would tell her story and save another girl from experiencing what she went through.

"My first attempt at the documentary happened in my final year of college but it wasn't very good. I put it aside for a few years and when my grandmother died, she made me promise to do it properly," Nic said, keeping her voice low. "To do that, I need funds."

Brooks was quiet for a long time, but his eyes remained on her face and Nic felt like she could see into his soul. "If you didn't need my money, if you didn't have a story to tell, you'd never consider marriage, would you?"

She wanted to be able to tell him that there was no way in hell she'd be marrying if it wasn't for Jane and the promise she made to her gran, but she couldn't deny the truth. There was a very good chance that, even without any incentive, she might've still said yes.

She was that attracted to him; her need to be with him, around him, superseded her good sense and any rational thought.

Instead of answering him—how could she admit that to him? It was hard enough facing the truth herself!—Nic leaned forward, her eyes on his lips. Placing her hand on his cheek, she rubbed her thumb through his stubble, loving the feel of his scruff beneath her fingers. Was she brave enough to kiss him, to find out how he tasted?

"Nic, would you have considered marriage to me?"

Knowing that he would push her for an answer, but not knowing why, Nic lowered his mouth to hers and when their lips met, a powder keg exploded beneath them. One minute she was kissing Brooks, her tongue gliding over his lips, and the next, she was straddling him, his hands on her bare ass and his tongue wrapped around hers, taking and giving and sucking...

And a minute later she was lying under him, his long form pressed into hers, her leg curled around his calf, her arm hooked around his neck as he kissed her and kissed her and kissed her...

Nic was lost in a vortex of need and passion and flat-out desire, but over her pounding heart she heard his soft whisper. "Would you have still considered marrying me, Nic?"

No, yes, she didn't know. Not having an answer, Nic just kissed him as the limousine made its way through Seattle's rain and fog to her front door.

After fleeing Napa Valley in Brooks's jet with Joshua, Teresa solemnly promised herself that she wouldn't sleep with Liam again, that she wouldn't allow him to mess with her head again.

Fail and fail.

When would she learn? Never, it seemed.

At the venue for the Ryan/Abbingdon wedding Teresa stepped onto the lavender-edged path that would take her to the bridal cottage and trailed her hand through the fragrant bushes.

Where was Liam now? What was he doing? She hadn't spoken to him since she'd stormed out of his office and while she had a bunch of questions for him—why had he proposed? Was his offer to loan her money against her shares still on the table? Did he really want to marry her?—she knew she had to stay away from him. Liam took up too much brain space and she'd needed to concentrate on Brooks and Nicolette's wedding. So she'd spent the past ten days working her ass off and the big day was finally here.

It was the most important day of her life, career-wise, and she couldn't afford to be distracted by thoughts of Liam Christopher and how much she missed him. Neither could she allow herself to be sidetracked by wondering and worrying about when she'd be contacted next about repaying Joshua's debt, trying to figure out why Linus left her the shares in the first place or the future of her business.

She could only worry about what she could control and this wedding should be—was, dammit!—her entire focus.

As she passed the groom's cottage, and the old-fashioned gazebo placed between the two cottages, she thought about Brooks's strange call the day before.

"There's something else I need you to do for me, Teresa."

Her toes had curled—not in a good way—at his greeting.

"Okay." Think about the money; think about the fact that organizing this wedding is a way to reestablish yourself.

"Can you delegate some of your pre-wedding duties to one or more of your minions, and help Nic dress?"

Nope. She liked Nicolette but they hardly knew each other. "I don't think Nicolette would want me to intrude…"

"She has no family and she works too hard to make friends." Yep, Teresa could relate. "I need you to be there, Teresa. I don't want her to be alone."

Hearing the concern in Brooks's voice had her, despite the millions of things she had to see to, saying yes.

Teresa looked over her shoulder toward the main buildings and sighed at how picture-perfect the venue looked. Using Brooks's money and influence, she'd persuaded the owner of The Two Barns, a fantastically exclusive wedding venue on the outskirts of Seattle, to speed up the last few renovations so that Brooks and Nic could hold their wedding in the newly converted, cathedral-like barns.

The smaller barn was a chapel and the bigger barn would hold the reception. The venue, with its old bridge, babbling stream and a profusion of weeping willows, was ridiculously pretty and also housed an award-winning restaurant on the premises. Joaquin, the Michelin-starred chef and owner, had also added two small cottages, places where the bridal parties could dress.

She'd love to wander around the grounds, sit next to the brook, dip her toes in the cool water. Pretend that her life wasn't going to hell in a broken-down wagon. She wanted a minute to catch her breath, to zone out, to center herself before she faced the madness of the next six to eight to ten hours. But because Brooks asked her to, she was going to check on the bride, hold her hand. See if she was okay...

The thing was, *she* wasn't okay. She was stressed and tired and unhappy, feeling isolated and a little scared, and very much alone, but she'd never, not in a million years, let Nicolette see that. This was her day to feel like a princess and she didn't need to know that her event planner felt like her nervous breakdown was waiting for her around the corner.

Teresa dug deep for her courage—that well was starting to run dry—and knocked on the cottage door. When she heard Nicolette's call to enter, she stepped into the exquisitely decorated room. Mint green and cream, feminine furnishings, sophisticated art. An unopened bottle of champagne stood in an ice bucket, and a plate of chocolate-tipped strawberries sat next to the bridal bouquet on the coffee table.

The room also contained one of the most beautiful brides she'd ever seen.

Teresa stopped, placed her hand on her heart and simply stared at the vision in front of her. Beaded silk flowers bloomed down a low bodice and along illusion tulle sleeves. The material gathered at her tiny waist, and expensive lace fell in a waterfall of fabric hand-beaded with pearls, beads and stones. A dramatic train completed her fairy-tale look.

Nicolette turned and lifted her eyebrows. "Do I look okay?"

"You look absolutely amazing," Teresa replied, feeling a little weepy. She'd done hundreds of weddings and rarely felt emotional, but Nicolette's ethereal, natural beauty took her breath away. And, truth be told, she was a little envious. She wanted to be Nicolette, who had an amazing career and was about to embark on this amazing life with a sexy, nice man. Nicolette didn't have to worry about her brother, his debts or deal with inconvenient feelings for a complicated man.

She wanted this, Teresa reluctantly admitted. She wanted the pretty dress, the flawless makeup, the bouquets of lilies sitting on the coffee table. She wanted a new start with a strong man...

She didn't want a half-assed proposal, nor did she

want a marriage based on convenience and protection and money and shares.

Teresa shook off her blues. "Brooks asked me to check on you. He wanted to make sure that you were all right."

Nicolette's eyes softened. "He's a good guy."

Teresa flashed her a grin. "And he's sexy as hell."

Nicolette smiled. "Isn't he just?"

Teresa sat down on the arm of the sofa and crossed her legs. She glanced at her watch and realized that it was later than she thought, fifteen minutes before Nicolette had to walk down the aisle. But they had time for a quick chat, a small glass of champagne. When she made the offer to Nicolette, she shook her head. "With my luck, I'll probably pour it over my dress."

Teresa looked longingly at the imported, expensive bottle of champagne. "And I'm working. Damn."

Standing, she walked over to the table and picked up a strawberry and popped it into her mouth. She moaned as the flavors hit her tongue. Ripe, juicy berries and dark, rich Belgian chocolate. Could she just stay here for the rest of the day and drink champers and gorge on strawberries and chocolate and pretend the real world didn't exist?

She wished.

"Those look amazing," Nicolette commented, looking at the strawberries with undisguised longing.

A girl should be able to eat whatever the hell she wanted to on her wedding day. Teresa picked up a berry by the stalk. "Open wide," Teresa commanded her.

"My dress, my makeup," Nicolette protested.

"Just bend forward and open up wide."

Nicolette did as she was told and Teresa popped the berry into her mouth, watching as her eyes fogged over with pleasure. "Aren't they divine?"

She nodded enthusiastically, chewed and opened her mouth again. Teresa fed her strawberries until Nicolette indicated that she'd had enough. "Thanks, I didn't have breakfast," Nic said. "Nerves."

"Can't think why you are nervous. You're only getting married today," Teresa quipped.

"I'm such a wuss." Nicolette's tone was desert-dry.

Teresa checked her watch again and tapped her foot. She shouldn't ask her this, she really shouldn't. "Nicolette, how did you know Brooks was the one?"

"Please call me Nic."

Her eyes flashed with an emotion Teresa couldn't identify. Then she dropped her eyes and looked away. Curious.

"I think that love, true love, ferocious love, doesn't roll around often and that, as a society, we are in love with the idea of love."

So that was a helluva complicated answer to a simple question.

"Love doesn't have to be the only reason for marriage, Teresa." Nic lifted one lovely, creamy shoulder. "I'm a practical person, Teresa, as I suspect are you."

Oh, damn, that had to mean that Nic was marrying Brooks for a reason other than love. Sadness swept over her. She liked Nic a lot and she liked Brooks, as well, and if they didn't marry for love, would they spend the rest of their lives feeling cheated? Because, if she had to marry Liam without love, her life would be sheer hell.

She'd saved herself; maybe she could save Nic, as well. "Please don't, Nic."

Nic lifted perfectly arched eyebrows. "Please don't what?"

"Marry him."

Realizing what she was putting at risk—her reputation as a wedding planner, the plans she had for that money, Joshua's hide—Teresa suddenly felt sick. What the hell was she doing? Was she certifiably insane?

But just like she and Liam did, Nicolette and Brooks deserved the ferocity of love, deserved happy-ever-after happiness. "You don't need to get married today. You can take your time, think this through."

Nic smiled softly. "Teresa, we have hundreds of guests waiting for me. We have spent a ridiculous amount of money—your fees included—to throw this function together in two weeks. Brooks is expecting me."

Teresa chewed the lipstick off her bottom lip. "It's the rest of *your* life, Nic. The rest of *his* life."

Nic ran her hand up Teresa's arm. "I'm not asking you to get married."

No, she wasn't, and she had no right to project her fears onto Nic. To judge her for what she was doing just because she couldn't marry without love and commitment and trust. She wanted it all; maybe Nic didn't need it. Nic took her hand and squeezed. "I know what I'm doing, Teresa."

"Of course you do. I'm sorry. I was out of line."

Nic cocked her head, her smile a little cheeky. "Why, Teresa St. Claire, I think you are a bit of a romantic."

"Maybe," Teresa reluctantly agreed.

Nic laughed softly and picked up the heavy skirts of luscious wedding dress. She nodded toward her cascading bouquet. "Can you grab that?"

Dammit, she was doing this. She really was. Nic walked toward the door and Teresa followed.

Teresa ran her hand across her eyes and sighed. *Not your circus, not your monkeys.* If Nic wanted to sacrifice herself on the altar of a marriage for any reason at all, big or small, it had nothing to do with her.

But she wouldn't do it; she couldn't do it. She'd love to marry Liam, but not like this. Never like this.

At the door, Nic took her bouquet and smoothed down her skirts. She sucked in a big breath and looked Teresa in the eye. "I'll be fine."

Teresa nodded. Leaning forward, she placed her cheek against Nic's. "I know."

Nic put a camera-ready, confident smile on her face. "Let's go give Brooks his birthday present."

It was Brooks's birthday? "It's his birthday today? What are you giving him as a gift?"

Nic's answer was short. And to the point. "Me."

Eight

If he never had to attend another wedding again it would be too soon. Liam, having arrived too late to watch the ceremony, walked into the reception and released a low whistle. He'd grown up with wealth, had attended far too many society events and weddings, but this venue was impressive.

The recently restored barn boasted clear grain cedar wallboards, high cathedral ceilings with polished beams and what he thought might be an original fir floor. The warmth of the wood was contrasted with a floor-to-ceiling glass wall on one end. The wood and glass effect was softened by a profusion of multicolored and massive flower arrangements and fairy lights. It was soft and elegant and pretty and, yeah, romantic.

Teresa was good at her job.

Liam ordered a Manhattan from a passing waiter, greeted an acquaintance and looked around for someone he'd like to talk to. Matt was across the room, waiting to issue his congratulations to the bridal couple. Brooks looked like another guy in his tuxedo and solid black tie but Nic, Liam admitted, looked like a fairy-tale princess in her gown. No wonder Brooks couldn't keep his eyes off his beautiful bride...

It was all so damn pretty and perfect. But marriage seldom was. Hadn't he seen this, not only with his parents, but also with dozens of acquaintances over the years? He'd attend the engagement parties and the weddings and six months later, a year, sometimes five, he'd hear that they were splitting, that they'd made a mistake. That divorce was inevitable.

And then he'd hear about the vicious divorce proceedings, the custody battles and he'd remember the pretty and perfect. It was all such...crap.

He'd watched and learned and rarely—okay never—allowed emotions to factor into his brief relationships. He'd never intended to get married, to put his head in that noose...

Yet, that was exactly what he'd proposed—marriage—and Teresa had been clever enough to say no. Marriage would never work between them; he was too reticent and Teresa was too independent. They were both too scarred and too scared.

Over the past ten days he'd spent a lot of time thinking about his crazy suggestion. Wondering why he'd made the offer. He finally, reluctantly, admitted that while he wanted to place Teresa under his protection—the protection of the Christopher name—he'd also wanted to save himself from being alone.

During that board meeting, with Teresa sitting in the seat next to him, knowing that she was there and solidly on his side, he'd felt stronger and more confident than he had in years. He'd felt invincible and he wanted the feeling to stick around.

If they married, he'd never have to attend another wedding or event alone; he wouldn't have to come home to a cold, silent, empty house. He'd have access to amazing sex with a partner he craved, whose body he adored.

He wouldn't be alone…

Nope, not a good enough reason to get hitched.

Liam looked around for the object of his thoughts and dreams, and the reason for his confusion. He doubted he'd find her; there were over five hundred people here and she'd be working behind the scenes to make sure that this event went off smoothly. Because, honestly, any mishap today would end her career. She'd had a few chances but if something happened to throw the wedding into disarray—whether it was her fault or not—Teresa would be persona very non grata in Seattle. Forever.

Liam looked around again, checking for threats he couldn't, admittedly, identify. He saw a young man to the left and his heart rate picked up. Was that Joshua, Teresa's brother? Looking again, Liam realized that the kid was too young, too fair, and he told himself to calm the hell down.

Taking his drink, he stared out the glass wall to the trees beyond the stream and thought that it would be a wonderful place for the paparazzi to hide, telescopic lenses poking out from between the branches of the trees. Had Teresa thought about that? Brooks would be pissed if unauthorized photos of his wedding hit the wire...

"Will you please stop scowling?"

Liam turned to see Matt with Nadia, as per usual, tucked into his side. They looked happy, content. Maybe, just maybe, Matt and Nadia would avoid the separation and the contentious divorce. He really hoped so. He liked them both, liked the way they looked together.

"Are you okay, Liam?" Nadia asked after kissing his cheek.

"Fine, thanks, Nadia." Liam forced some joviality into his tone and decided to tease Matt. "When are you going to ditch this this ugly and poor dude, Nadia? You can do so much better."

Nadia's mouth pursed and she looked like she was considering his suggestion. "Tempting but...no." Nadia looked across the room, waved at someone and stepped away from Matt. "I'll leave you two to chat. I've seen someone I want to have a word with."

Matt watched Nadia walk away with a sappy look on his face. The man was toast. And he looked happy being toast. God help him.

"Quite a party," Matt commented.

"Yep. I hope everyone enjoyed watching Brooks

while he had his spine and balls removed. Hope he gets some kick-ass presents for his trouble."

Matt narrowed his eyes. "Hell, that's cold and cynical, even for you, man."

Remorse rolled over Liam, cold and greasy. Sighing, he rubbed the back of his neck and softly swore. "Sorry. Being here makes me feel scratchy."

He and Matt were best friends but he couldn't tell him that he wanted what Matt had, having a woman in his life who was there for him, only for him. Someone whom he could trust, love, rely on.

Liam couldn't look at Matt—he didn't want to see the pity on his face and looked toward the glass end wall and there she was, dressed in a halter-neck emerald jumpsuit, looking tall and willowy and so sexy it hurt. Liam immediately felt the ache in his heart and the hitch in his breath. Teresa's hair was pulled into a loose knot at the back of her neck—no surprise there—and, because she was holding an iPad, everyone knew she was working but she still looked effortlessly classy.

He wanted her. Would there ever be a time when he didn't? Liam doubted it.

Teresa's eyes met his and even though they were so far apart, he could see the sadness in her eyes. Why couldn't they make this work? Why was it hard? Why wasn't sex enough?

Why did he, more than anything, want to take her in his arms and slow-dance her around the room? For the rest of his life?

And because the thought was knock-him-off-his-feet

powerful and equally terrifying, Liam handed Matt his drink and walked toward the exit and toward the valet parking. Ten minutes later he was in his car, speeding back to the city.

Nicolette swallowed another yawn and resisted the urge to lean her head on Brooks's very broad, very comfortable shoulder. They were seated at the wedding table and Nic thought that she finally, finally, had a minute alone with her, *gulp*, new husband. Before either of them had a chance to speak, Brooks's grandfather—white-haired, white-mustached and bearer of the plummiest of plummy English accents—pulled up a chair next to them and Nic swallowed her frustrated growl.

"Happy birthday, son."

Nicolette placed her elbow on the table and her chin in her hands. At the altar, she'd whispered a quiet happy birthday to Brooks when she reached his side and, as long as she lived, she'd never forget the emotion in his Cognac-colored eyes: lust and pride and…affection?

"You're the best birthday present I've ever received," Brooks told her and then he smiled at her and she all but melted at his feet.

Nic gave herself a mental slap and reminded herself that he'd most likely been thinking about the money that was, probably, already lodged in his bank account. The money he needed to take complete control of Abbingdon Airlines.

This wasn't a fairy tale and Brooks wasn't about

to pluck stars from the sky and hand them to her. Despite her glorious dress and the pretty flowers and the amazing food and venue—Teresa had cemented her reputation as one of the best event coordinators in the city—this wedding was still a sham, a short-lived arrangement. She couldn't afford to forget that.

And she couldn't allow her full-blown, very grown-up and kick-ass attraction to her brand-new husband to complicate this imbroglio any further. Imbroglio, what a lovely word...

"So marriage plus your birthday must mean that you have liquidated your trust fund," Lester said.

Brooks's expression turned inscrutable and Nic noticed his grim smile. "As we sit here, a formal offer to buy your shares in Abbingdon Airlines is winging its way to your inbox. In terms of our agreement, you have to accept my offer."

"Yes, I saw that."

Brooks pushed his hand through his hair. "I don't mean to bring up an old argument but I really think you investing in that hotel chain is a very bad idea."

"So you've said." Lester sipped his drink and regarded Brooks over the rim. "Okay, I'll take your advice and not invest."

If she wasn't absolutely wiped and feeling equally overwhelmed, Nic might've smiled at Brooks's astonishment. She figured it didn't happen very often. "What?"

"You're better at business than I am. Since I no longer need all your millions, would you like them back? As a wedding present?"

Brooks's mouth fell open and he glanced at the glass in Lester's hand. "How many of those have you had?" he demanded.

"Enough." Lester drained his drink and pushed himself to his feet. Ignoring Brooks's suspicious expression, he picked up Nic's hand and dropped an old-fashioned kiss on her knuckles.

"You are truly lovely, Nicolette. I look forward to getting to know you better." Lester squeezed her hand and sent her a soft smile. "You've married the best of us, my dear. Welcome to the family."

Lester drifted off and Brooks's eyes followed his progress across the room. When Lester disappeared, he looked at Nic, lifted his hands and shook his head. "What the hell—"

Nic lifted her hand to her mouth to hide her yawn. "Problem?"

Brooks frowned. "On the surface, no. But I think I've just been thoroughly outmaneuvered by that wily old fox."

Okay, she was battling to keep up. "I don't understand."

His smile was a mixture of ruefulness and amusement. "I don't think he ever intended to invest. This was all about getting me married."

Nic wanted to pay attention, she really did, but she felt her eyes closing and when Brooks cupped her cheek into his hand, she sighed. If he just held her head, just like that, she could probably sleep. Yeah, that would go down well with his friends and business associates. She could see the headlines…

BORED ALREADY? ABBINGDON'S NEW WIFE FALLS ASLEEP AT WEDDING TABLE.

Nic straightened her spine and rolled her head to release some knots. She knew that Brooks was staring at her but she couldn't meet his eyes, fearing that he would see how much she wanted him, how much she ached to take this evening to its natural conclusion. Back to business, chick. "Right, who else should we talk to?"

Brooks gripped her chin and tipped it up, forcing Nic to meet his eyes. Warm eyes, eyes the color of burned sugar. "I just want to sit here and look at you," Brooks said, his deep voice soft and sensuous. "You look absolutely exquisite, Nic."

Nic's hand drifted over her full skirt. "Thank you. You look pretty good yourself."

He snorted. "I'm just a guy in a tux. You, on the other hand, look perfect."

She wanted to believe him, she did, but she didn't want to set herself up to feel disappointed. She liked Brooks. God help her if she fell in love with him.

Brooks pushed back the sleeve of his jacket to reveal the simple face of what she assumed to be a very expensive watch. Brooks lifted one strong eyebrow. "Want to get out of here?"

She very much did. She wanted a hot shower, to wash her hair and brush her teeth and collapse in a heap. Nic just nodded.

Brooks stood up, took her hand and pulled back her chair. Nic rose and sighed when she saw a well-known, very charismatic senator heading in their direction. Brooks ran his thumb over her cheekbone and placed his hand on her hip, pulling her close. Nic held her breath, thinking he was about to kiss her and ignored her disappointment when his lips brushed her ear. "Excuse yourself to go to the bathroom. Wait five minutes and when you leave, turn right down the passage instead of left. There's an emergency exit and there's a car waiting there for you."

Oh, that sounded like heaven. She could, absolutely, do that. But…what then? Where would she go? Where should she go? Back to her house, back to his? Nicolette hadn't thought of what would happen after they said their I-do's but she didn't want this evening to end.

Brooks brushed her lips once, then twice, and Nic heard his frustrated sigh. "Bathroom, emergency exit, limo."

Nic took the moment—she shouldn't have but she did—and slapped her lips on his in a hard, desperate kiss. As she walked away, she felt his eyes on her back and forced herself not to turn around and bellow her burning questions across the room.

What now? Where am I going? Am I going to see you later?

Nic wrapped her arms around her pillow and, smelling the sea, opened her eyes. A sheer curtain fluttered in the window as a warm wind rushed over her face and shoulders, before picking up and blowing the fabric to one side. Nic gasped as she caught a glimpse of a sparkling infinity pool and beyond

that, a blue-green ocean. Sitting up, Nic looked down
and saw that she was dressed in an oversize T-shirt.
Then she saw the wedding band on her finger and
her eyes darted to the ring finger on her right hand
to the spectacular ring Brooks placed there when she
agreed to marry him.

She was married to Brooks; she remembered the
wedding. Nic wrapped her arms around her knees,
yawned and recalled Brooks sliding into the limo next
to her and his brief order to his driver to take them to
the airport. Fighting sleep—by that point she'd been
beyond exhaustion—she'd asked her new husband
where they were going.

She vaguely recalled him saying something about
a no-strings honeymoon, that she should sleep and
when he'd tapped his shoulder, suggesting that she
rest her head against it, she had. He'd carried her on
his plane and placed her on a bed in the private cabin.
She'd apparently, somehow, slept through the flight
and the drive from the airport to…wherever this was.

Flinging back the sheet, Nic padded across the
room to the veranda and stepped onto an expansive
balcony. Walking past the infinity pool, she stopped
at the tempered glass that served as a wall and looked
down. Nic sucked in her breath at the thirty-meter
drop on the other side of the barrier. The cliff ended
in a small, white, what looked to be private, beach.

And then beyond that, a hundred yards of shallow,
crystal-clear, blue sea. So…

Wow.

"Morning, sleepyhead."

Nic smiled at his low, deep voice and slowly turned. Brooks was lying on a lounger under the shade of an umbrella, wearing designer sunglasses and a pair of plain black swimming shorts. He was also wearing miles and miles of tawny skin covering big, defined muscles. Oh, God, she'd known that he was in shape but hadn't thought he'd have such muscled legs, big arms and a washboard stomach.

Nic pushed her hand into what she knew was messy hair and wished that she'd taken the time to shower, to brush her teeth. He looked like chocolate-covered sin and she…

Didn't.

"Hi." Nic sent a longing look to the room she left and wondered if he'd think she was nuts if she bolted back inside and hit the shower. Probably. Definitely. Nic, knowing that she couldn't keep staring at him—oh, how she wanted to!—looked at the blindingly white house behind them before gesturing to the sea. "Where are we?"

"St. Barts. This is one of the Abbingdon vacation homes."

One of their homes? "How many do you have?"

Brooks pushed his sunglasses to rest on top of his head. "A few." Those rich eyes drifted over her in frank admiration. "You're looking so much better. You were totally out of it for a while."

Nic colored. "I haven't slept much lately. I suppose it all caught up with me. And when I did sleep, I didn't get any rest."

"Did the thought of marrying me give you night-mares?" Brooks asked, swinging his feet to the floor.

She couldn't tell him that she was terrified of fall-ing in love with him, petrified that one day, probably sooner rather than later, she'd have to walk away from him after sampling a taste of what life with Brooks was like. Oh, the wealth was...nice, she supposed, but if he lost everything tomorrow, she knew that she'd still want to wake up to his beautiful eyes, that hard body, that slow smile.

Man, how was she going to resist him? Seeing that he was still waiting for an answer, Nic shrugged. "Change is always scary."

"It can be. It can also be exciting and thrilling and life-changing," Brooks quietly stated, standing up. "Well, we're here for a week and there's not a hell of a lot to do besides tan and swim and snorkel. I need to work for a few hours but I could also do with some downtime."

A week on the beach? It sounded like heaven. There was only one thing that would make it better...

Don't, Nic, it's not a good idea.

He said that it was a no-strings honeymoon, that he didn't expect anything. Actually, she remembered hearing a great deal of hope in his voice but that might've been extreme tiredness causing her imagina-tion to run riot. There was only one way to find out...

If you sleep with him, it'll be so much harder to walk away.

But if I don't sleep with him I might lose my mind.

"Do you want me?"

Oh, God, she'd intended those words to come out smooth and a little carefree, not desperate and demanding. He was going to think she was as gauche as a teenager...

When it came to Brooks Abbingdon, she was.

Brooks tensed and his head snapped up and his gaze pinned her to the floor. He swallowed and when he spoke, Nic heard the rough edge in his normally smooth voice. "I want you so much I can barely breathe."

Phew. Well...

Good.

Brooks stayed where he was, his arms folded against his chest, his fingers digging into his biceps. Why wasn't he moving? Didn't he understand what she was offering? Nic lifted her thumb to gnaw the edge of a nonexistent cuticle. "Um...well...crap, I don't know what to say now."

"You could say that you want me, too," Brooks stated but Nic heard a touch of insecurity underneath his evenly stated words.

"I thought that was as obvious as a sixty-foot flashing neon sign," Nic admitted. "That's a big part of why I haven't been sleeping."

"Because you've been thinking about me?"

Nic blushed but nodded. "There have been a couple of dreams that have been real and I wake up, hovering on the edge of..." She stumbled over her words and waved her hand. "Oh, God, shut up now, Nic."

"I'd really prefer that you didn't," Brooks said, amusement in his eyes. And then he, finally, started to move. Nic watched his long-legged stride, saw the erection pulling his trunks tight, and wondered where all the saliva in her mouth had gone.

When he was a few feet from her, Nic held up her hand. "This has nothing to do with anything else, our fake marriage or our business arrangement."

"We left that behind in Seattle," Brooks agreed. "All of it. It's just me, Brooks, desperate to kiss you, Nic."

She wanted that, too, wanted his mouth on hers… oh, yuck! Her mouth! Ack!

Nic slapped her hand over her mouth and saw Brooks's eyes widen. He stopped and lifted an eyebrow. "And now?" he asked.

"I need a shower and to brush my teeth." Nic mumbled the words against the palm of her hand.

Brooks smiled at her and he looked ten years younger. Bending his knees, he placed his shoulder against her stomach and wrapped one arm around her bare thighs. Hoisting her up and over his shoulder, he patted her satin-covered butt and walked her down the veranda toward the far end of the house. As he stepped into an expansive master suite, Nic saw that the room was at the end of the house and was open on two sides. The view from this room was more stunning, if that was at all possible, than the view from her room.

Her heart pounding and her temperature rising, but that could be because Brooks's hand had sneaked between the tops of her thighs, she was carried by Brooks as he walked her past a massive bed and into an open-air bathroom. Allowing her to slide down his body, oh, wow, he was hot and hard…everywhere, Brooks turned her to face one of the two basins. Rummaging in the cupboard below, he pulled out a brand-new toothbrush and removed it from its packaging. Handing her the brush and a tube of toothpaste, he told her she had two minutes.

Fascinated by the need in his eyes, and the way he kept looking at her mouth, Nic obeyed. She couldn't wait to kiss him…

Brooks left her and walked over to the open-air double-headed shower, encased by the same tempered clear glass barrier she'd seen earlier on the entertainment area. Her mouth full of toothpaste, Nic looked past Brooks onto a thick forest below and realized it was totally private.

Yay, because she had a feeling that her back and ass were going to be wedged against that glass as Brooks slid into her.

Damn, she really couldn't wait. Like not for one second more.

Nine

She was absolutely not going to get naked with Liam this morning. This was a business meeting, a follow-up meeting—as he'd stated in his email, asking her to carve out some time for him—not a let's-get-naked meeting.

Not that she had many—or any—problems getting naked with Liam Christopher.

"It's nine o'clock on Monday morning for God's sake," Teresa muttered to herself.

Duncan, Liam's sharply dressed PA, looked up from his monitor and lifted a perfectly groomed eyebrow. And that reminded her; she needed to book a facial and a brow shaping, a mani and pedi. With her hectic schedule lately organizing Brooks and Nic's wedding, she hadn't had any time for herself.

Oh, and a bikini wax was also needed. Now, there was a very decent reason why, when she was finally admitted into Liam's inner sanctum, she'd keep all her clothes on.

Duncan leaned back in his chair and offered a pleasant greeting. "Liam said you did a spectacular job organizing the Ryan/Abbingdon wedding. He was very impressed."

Teresa felt like she'd won the lottery and had to stop herself from dancing on the spot. Then cynicism rolled in... Liam wasn't the type who handed out praise easily. "Did he really say that or are you just being nice?"

Duncan rolled his eyes. "He really said that."

Oh.

Oh, wow. Liam liked what she did. And if he liked it, then maybe the rest of Seattle did, too, and she'd start picking up work again. Because she still had her brother's hide to save and his debt to repay.

Duncan stood up and walked around his desk. Taking Teresa's arm, he pulled her over to his desk and pointed at a small box with a green and a red light on it. "When the green light flicks on, you can go on in." Duncan straightened his tie. "I'm going to organize coffee because I'm pretty sure you're all going to need some." He pulled a face. "That or a fire extinguisher."

Teresa watched him walk away, conscious of the fire in her cheeks. She hoped that Duncan wasn't referring to what happened the last time she and Liam were alone together. How would he even know that they'd made love? Had the words "just got laid" appeared on her forehead as she left Liam's office?

Now, there was just one more reason why no clothes would be shed during this meeting. Not a tie, not even her jacket…it was a slippery slope and she had no intention of ending up in a tangled, bruised and bloody heap at the bottom of the hill. Because, yeah, that was exactly what was going to happen if she didn't get her feelings for Liam under control. Though, honestly, that horse might've already bolted.

Like, weeks ago…

The light on Duncan's desk flashed green and Teresa strode over to his door, pushing down on the ornate handle. It would be better to get ahead of their attraction, to remind him this was a business meeting and that it was Monday morning. It was the most sensible, businesslike time of the week and that was what they had to be. Businesslike.

"I have half an hour for you, and all of those thirty minutes will be spent with our clothes on."

Teresa saw Liam's grin and out of the corner of her eye she saw a flutter of a cream silk skirt, the flash of a peach blouse.

Oh, shit, they weren't alone.

Teresa, her cheeks flaming, turned her head and…

Yep. Liam's mother, her expression perfectly haughty, sat on his expensive sofa, the same sofa on which Liam had loved her so well.

Gah.

"Mrs. Christopher, I didn't know…ah…" Teresa

sent a helpless look at Liam, looking stupidly sexy in a deep gray suit and bottle-green tie.

"Teresa, you remember my mother, Catherine," Liam smoothly stated, walking around his desk to gently grip her biceps. "My mother stopped by but she's about to leave."

Feeling steadier, she was shocked when Liam's mouth drifted across hers. "Hi," he murmured.

Teresa's eyes immediately flew back to Catherine's eating-a-sour-lemon face.

Deep in her tote bag, her phone rang and, deeply thankful for the interruption, Teresa dived into it, keeping her face down to give herself time to think. It was obvious that Catherine Christopher still blamed her for the breakup of her marriage, and was, obviously, still incensed that Linus left her twenty-five percent of his shares in this business. As for her baby sleeping with her archenemy? If looks could kill, she'd be a tiny pile of ash on Liam's expensive carpet.

Teresa uttered her standard greeting. Hopefully, it would be a client and she could use him, or her, as an excuse to skedaddle.

"Teresa, they've found me!"

Dammit, dammit, dammit. She'd left her phone on loudspeaker and her brother's voice bounced off Liam's office walls.

"Josh, hold on," Teresa commanded him, punching the button to make their conversation private.

Turning her back on the mother and son duo, she walked past Liam's desk to the window, placing her hand on the glass and keeping her voice low. "What happened?"

"I got a call at The Bridge. We're not supposed to have them but they let me take it," Joshua shouted, his voice sounding like a hundred decibels in her ear. Teresa's blood froze. She'd booked Josh in under an assumed name, paid in cash. He shouldn't have been found, not this quickly.

Stay calm, Teresa. You have to think. "What did they say?"

"That I had a week to pay up. That if not, I was dead, and you were, too."

Teresa closed her eyes and rested her forehead on the glass. She sent Liam a quick look and caught the concern in his eyes. "Okay, that's doable. I can raise the money and we'll put an end to this."

"Where will you get the money?"

Did it matter? "Where are you now?" Teresa asked, avoiding his question.

"I snuck out and am back in the city. I went by your apartment and picked up my phone," Joshua replied. "Where are you going to get the money, Teresa?"

"Why does it matter, Joshua? The debt will be paid."

Joshua waited a beat before replying. "Because I was told that if you take the money from Liam Christopher, we'll still die. And so will Christopher."

Teresa felt her knees buckle, her throat tighten. "That makes no sense," she whispered. "Why do they care where the money comes from?"

"I don't know but they do," Joshua replied. "So

guess we are back to square one, right? What are we going to do...run?".

Liam was her only option for money and if she couldn't borrow it from him—and there was no way that she'd put his life in danger—they'd have to. "I'll meet you at home, Josh."

"Yeah. But later." Josh disconnected the call and Teresa released a howl. Frustrated beyond belief, her stress levels climbing, Teresa banged her phone against the window.

Liam plucked the phone from her grasp and pulled her into his arms, cradling her head against his chest.

Teresa wanted to wrap her arms around his waist, sink into his strength but she couldn't. He was now in the crosshairs of the same people targeting them, and she would not put him in danger. There had been too many casualties in this war; she was damned if Liam was going to be one, too. She could not risk his life by borrowing money against her shares, by having anything more to do with him. He was too precious, too important...

Liam had been her only option for quick money and now there was no way she'd be able to raise seven million in less than a week. And judging by the threats, it seemed that the people holding Joshua's marker weren't interested in a pay-back-in-installments arrangement.

By calling Josh, threatening him, they were telling her that they could find him, them, if they tried to hide. If they wanted a shot at safety, they'd needed another plan.

As Joshua suggested, they'd have to run, to leave the west coast, find new identities and get used to a life on the run. It was the only way they'd survive.

If they survived.

Teresa's mind raced. She had the money Brooks paid her; she hadn't paid her suppliers yet. Yeah, if she didn't pay them, she'd be stealing, defrauding them, but she needed every cent of that payout from Brooks to get them new identities, to purchase a car for cash, to pay for flights to somewhere else…

Her business, and her reputation, would never survive but if they didn't run, neither would they.

It was the only option they had left. Teresa, sucking in every last bit of courage she possessed, placed her hands on Liam's chest and pushed herself out of his arms. Without looking at him—she couldn't because if she did, she'd beg him for help and then he'd be in danger—she held out her hand for her phone.

"I've got to go. I'll call you in a few hours."

"Stay here, Teresa. Let me help you," Liam said, his voice low and persuasive.

"I'll reschedule," Teresa lied. What she'd do, once they were on the road, is find a lawyer and sign over all her shares to him even though the year wasn't up. Yeah, she'd lose the money but it would sever the tie between them. He'd be safe and if she and Josh wanted to survive the next few months, years, decades, she needed to cut her ties with everyone.

Giving up everyone and everything would be the price she'd have to pay for her, Josh and, most important, Liam, to stay alive.

So be it.

Teresa stood up on her tiptoes and brushed her mouth against Liam's, leaving it there for a moment longer than appropriate. How could she walk away from him? Where was she going to find the strength? She wanted to tell him she loved him, that he was everything she'd ever wanted, or needed. That his was the head she wanted sharing her pillow, the body she wanted to wake up beside, the smile she wanted to see when she was eighty. The hand she wanted to hold when death came calling.

"Let me help you," Liam repeated, his fingers digging into her hips.

Teresa forced a smile on her lips. "With what, Liam?" she said, keeping her voice chirpy. "All is well."

"Don't lie to me," Liam said.

Teresa bit her bottom lip, cursing the tears that filled her eyes. "Then don't ask me questions that require a lie." Teresa stood on her toes, kissed his cheek and pulled back. "Bye, Liam."

Teresa forced herself to walk to the door, forced her leaden feet to move. Ignoring Catherine, who watched their interactions with undisguised glee, she finally—finally—reached the door.

"Don't make me come after you, Teresa," Liam warned.

Teresa looked back at him and the tears she'd tried so hard to contain, rolled down her face. "Please don't, Liam. I'm just going to say no."

Liam wore his stubborn expression and Teresa knew what to say to stop him from chasing after her. She would have to force the words out but they were words she knew would keep him away, words that would keep him safe. Because his safety was all that mattered.

Teresa tossed her hair and prepared to utter her biggest lie ever. The one she knew would burn every bridge between them.

"I should never have slept with your dad."

Teresa saw the pain flash in Liam's eyes and forced herself to remain upright. She couldn't fall to the floor; she had too much to do.

Forcing a smile onto her face took everything she had. "He was good but you are better."

"You bitch! You slutty, skanky trollop. I was right! I am always right!"

Teresa pulled the door closed on Catherine's vitriol, knowing that Liam's mother would never be a fan.

What really hurt was that, after today, Liam wouldn't be, either.

That was good for his safety, bad for her.

As long as Liam was safe, she could live with just about anything.

She was lying through her pretty, pearly teeth. And badly, at that.

Liam looked at his closed door and shook his head. Teresa hadn't slept with his father; any fool could see that she'd uttered those words to distance herself from him, to put an insurmountable barrier between them. She'd only say something like that to make him so mad that he'd wash his hands of her.

Well, tough crap, lady. It wasn't working. He wasn't that thick or that easily manipulated. Or weak.

"I told you she slept with your father! Why won't anyone listen to me?"

Catherine's high-pitched scream pierced his what-the-hell moment and Liam pulled his eyes off his door, resisting the urge to go after Teresa. Oh, she thought he was done, but she wasn't getting away from him that easily.

And he was done with her being stubborn, was sick of her pride and her need to fly solo. This situation needed to end. And it would, today.

Ignoring his mother, who'd moved on to her well-rehearsed diatribe about his father's unfaithfulness and how awful her life was, he pulled his phone from the inside pocket of his jacket and stared down at the screen. Relief rolled over him as he saw the text message on his phone. Somehow he'd had the presence of mind, while he'd had possession of Teresa's phone, to forward her brother's contact number to his phone.

And he knew just the guy who had the skills to tell him where exactly Joshua St. Claire was, right at this moment. Jeremy Dutton was more than just a private investigator. *Investigator* barely began to describe all the things Dutton was capable of.

Teresa wasn't the only one with a Fixer.

When Dutton answered, Liam didn't bother with niceties. "I need you to ping this number and find out exactly where this phone is," Liam said.

"How soon do you need it?" Dutton asked.

"Five minutes ago," Liam retorted.

"Okay, working on it."

"Also, I also need you to front me seven mil. I'll pay you back in a few days." Dutton was one of the few people who had tens of millions in cash he could easily access. Handy when people like him needed a lot of cash quickly. Dutton charged exorbitant rates for the temporary loan but Liam could afford it.

"Unmarked bills?"

"Preferably." Liam gripped the bridge of his nose, his mind turning over at warp speed. He quickly laid the bare facts on the table, reminding Dutton of Teresa's circumstances. He'd done the investigation on her, but Liam wasn't his only client, so a reminder brought him up to speed.

"I need you to contact the head of that organization and make arrangements for this debt to be settled. I want it done this afternoon. You will pay them directly and I want a guarantee that the association between them and the St. Claires will be terminated once that money changes hands. I want them to forget they ever heard their names."

"Why don't I secure world peace and reverse climate change while I'm at it?" Dutton grumbled.

"Are you not up to it? Shall I call The Fixer?"

Desperate times meant desperate measures and Liam knew that mentioning his competitor's name would motivate Dutton.

Liam saw his mother's shocked face and ignored her waving hands, her gestures to get him to stop talking. "I'm offering you another hundred thousand, on top of the interest you're charging on the loan, to make this all go away. But I want it done by this afternoon."

"Two-fifty."

Greedy bastard. "Two."

"Done. I'll let you know when the deal is completed."

"And get me the location of that phone."

"On it."

Liam disconnected the call and looked at his mother, who sat on the edge of her chair, looking ashen. "What's wrong with you?"

"You believe her," Catherine said, now sounding calm and utterly disconnected.

"Who are you talking about?" Liam demanded. He didn't have time for his mother right now. He needed to stop Teresa from doing whatever she was planning. Because she sure as hell was planning something.

"You are just like your father."

Liam's fingers returned to grip his nose as he looked for calm. There was a good chance that he might lose it with his mother today and it wasn't going to be pretty. Long overdue maybe, but not pretty.

Liam didn't have time to pussyfoot around Catherine. "What she said about sleeping with Dad, it was a lie, Mom. She never slept with him."

"She just admitted it!" Catherine screamed, pointing at the closed door.

"She was lying." Probably to protect him but he wasn't sure why. He didn't need it. But whatever her reasoning, her inability to ask for help annoyed and hurt him. But why was he surprised? Teresa did everything solo.

"I can't see the attraction! She's a piece of skirt, a tramp—"

"Be careful, Mother."

"No matter what I do, she still comes out smelling like a rose!"

Liam was about to ask his mother to leave when her words sank in.

He tensed as icy fingers of dread tap-danced on his spine. "What do you mean, no matter what you do?"

Please let her have misspoken; please let it not be what he was thinking.

Liam stared at Catherine and noticed the malevolence in her eyes. This was going to be a lot worse than what he thought.

Catherine, as defiant as hell, met his eyes. "She got her hooks into your father. I absolutely wasn't going to let her get her hooks into you."

"What did you do?" Liam dropped his voice, knowing that he had to keep a cap on his anger because, if he let it loose, it would roar and claw and eviscerate.

Catherine stood up and lifted her shoulders in an elegant, indifferent shrug. "I was the source of the tabloid rumors. I've been telling my friends, and encouraging them to tell their friends, not to hire Teresa St. Claire, that she's just not our sort."

Yeah, that was the truth; it just wasn't all the truth. "What else?"

That shrug again. He didn't want to think, or face

it, but he had to ask. "Did you have any interactions with her brother, Joshua?"

Catherine inspected her nails. "Not directly."

She wanted to tell him, he realized; she wanted him to know. To brag? He wouldn't put it past her. Liam remained quiet and waited her out. It didn't take long for her to start talking.

"When I heard that she was working for Matt, I knew that you'd run into her and I knew that there was a chance that you'd still find her attractive. I was soon proved right. I was not going to let her back into our lives."

Oh, shit.

"I'd always kept tabs on her. I thought it necessary. I knew exactly who she was, what her brother had done. I made contact with the people who bought her brother's debt and I encouraged them to inflate the interest, to apply pressure. I made certain financial contributions to make her life hell."

"Did you have anything to do with Joshua's flight across the country, him gate-crashing Matt's party?"

"A little ketamine, two thugs and a thousand dollars will go a long way," Catherine admitted without a shred of remorse. "I also fed the tabloids information and photographs about her affair with your father but I have to admit, that girl is harder to scare than I thought."

Liam realized that he'd never been this angry before. Right now he absolutely hated his mother. Loathed her with every fiber of his being.

He still had so many questions but he was running

out of time. "How did you contact the people holding Josh's debt?"

"The same way you did. People in our social circle, people with serious money, all have people who take care of things like that for us," Catherine replied, bored. "We don't do it ourselves, darling."

"The Fixer?"

"Someone like him." Liam fought the insane desire to laugh. People like them never got their hands dirty; they directed proceedings from afar. Plausible deniability, wasn't that the term? No more. He was done with trying to keep his hands clean. If fighting dirty was what was needed to save Teresa from his mother's machinations and, as scary, the criminal underworld, that was what he'd do.

Picking up his phone, he redialed the previous number he'd used.

"I just sent you the coordinates," Jeremy stated. "Since you're in your office, it should take you about ten minutes to get to him."

"I want to be in on those conversations. I want to be in on that meeting. I want to be the one to hand over the cash. Make it happen."

Liam looked at his mother and narrowed his eyes at her. He tossed his phone on his desk and sent his mother a hard look. "I want you out of my life, Catherine, but right now I'll settle for you leaving my office."

Catherine, for the first time in her life, left without further argument.

Ten

It took a few hours to track Joshua down as the kid kept moving through the city. When he did, Liam sat on the park bench next to Teresa's younger brother, watching him out of the corner of his eye. Joshua looked as relaxed as a rabbit on speed and at any moment he expected him to bolt. Liam, on hearing that Joshua was in Cal Anderson Park, was surprised to find him on one of the first benches after entering the park.

"Did my sister send you?" Joshua demanded.

"No, the world has to stop turning before your sister asks me for help," Liam muttered, still annoyed. "So, what's the plan? How are you going to deal with this situation? How do you plan on repaying the money?"

Joshua's expression turned grim. "We're not. If we

can't borrow it from you it leaves us only one option and that's to run."

Liam felt his heart constrict. Running was the stupidest idea ever. "Wait, back up. What do you mean if we can't borrow it from me?"

Joshua looked at him like he was thick. "Because if we do, we all die. Including you."

Nice. So that was the reason Teresa issued that stupid lie. She'd been trying to protect him.

Liam forced himself to push the thought of his imminent demise away. "That makes no sense. They shouldn't care where the money comes from, just that they get it. Unless…"

Unless his mother put that bug in their ear.

Oh, that sounded like something she'd say. Liam wanted to believe that she didn't mean it but, having seen what lengths she'd go to get Teresa out of his life, and hers, he wasn't so sure.

Dutton's voice flowed into his ear. "When I spoke to the boss, he made it clear that he's only concerned about getting the money asap. If that was a condition, he would've said something so I think it's safe to assume that they don't give a damn who pays and that it was an empty threat."

"Awesome," Liam replied to Dutton, who was monitoring his conversation through some fancy spy gear. He had a bud in his ear and the pen in his inside pocket was operating as a microphone and recorder. He was also somewhere around and when he met with his contact, Dutton would video-record the transaction. There was no way anyone would be able to dispute the payment.

Liam put his hand on the leather knapsack, needing to keep contact with the cash that had been delivered to his office an hour ago. Newish bills, packets and packets of them.

He was carrying around seven million dollars in cash and in thirty minutes, he was going to hand the rucksack over at a coffee shop not far from here. He was trying to play it cool but he hoped Joshua couldn't tell that his heart felt like it was about to beat out of his chest. It wasn't every day one met with the lieutenant of some mafia-like organization. Okay, he met with sharks all the time—his board members were an excellent example—but these were streetwise sharks and they had a history of drawing blood.

Joshua's phone rang and the kid leaped a foot out of his seat. He pulled it out of the deep pocket of his stupid, low-hanging pants—had he never heard of a belt?—and squinted at the display. "It's Teresa again. She's flipping out."

Liam hated the thought of Teresa worrying and could easily imagine her pacing her apartment, wondering where the hell Joshua was. But if she, and Joshua, were kept in the dark about what he was doing there was no chance of either of them messing up his plans. And Teresa wouldn't run without Joshua and he intended to keep Joshua with him until the very last minute.

This needed to end and he intended to do exactly that.

Joshua stared at his heavy biker boots. "Why are you doing this? Why are you helping me?"

Liam thought it better that there was no misunderstanding between him and Teresa's brother. "I'm not doing it for you."

Joshua frowned and for the first time, his eyes met Liam's. "Uh…you're not?"

Liam folded his arms across his chest. "Nope. I'm doing this for your sister, so that you can stop being the biggest pain in her ass."

"I…um… I know I messed up," Joshua hedged and his voice took on a whiny tinge that Liam despised.

"You are in your twenties, St. Claire. When are you going to stand on your own two feet and stop expecting your sister to bail your skinny ass out of trouble?"

"I didn't mean to—"

Liam plowed his fist into Joshua's biceps and the kid skidded down the park bench and nearly fell off the end. "Stop lying to yourself. You act first and think later or you ask Teresa to think for you. That stops here. And it stops today."

"I guess," Joshua muttered. "You're hella protective over my sister. Why are you doing this?"

"God alone knows."

Joshua tipped his head to the side. "Have you told my sister that you love her?"

Liam turned his head slowly and he saw Joshua inch down the bench, away from him. He wanted to deny his words but he couldn't; neither did he have an answer to his question. He hadn't told Teresa because, as of two seconds ago, he wasn't completely

sure that he did. Now he was. Sure, that is. She was
his; she always had been since that evening they first
met all those years ago.

He loved her.

That had to be the reason why he was handing over
seven million dollars to some assface at lunchtime on
a Monday morning.

"Well?" Joshua asked. "Does she know? Are you
ever going to tell her?"

Not yet, not quite yet. Maybe never. There were so
many gaps in his life, so many blanks he still needed
to fill. He needed those missing puzzle pieces to be
filled before he could go to Teresa and hand his
heart over. There were so many questions he needed
answered—about his parents, about why Linus left
her his shares—and he would also need to tell her
about Catherine's machinations.

His mother had messed with her and Joshua's
lives, had tried to ruin her business, caused her un-
told worry. How would she be able to look past that
to a life with him?

She'd thought that she was bad for him but today's
events proved that he wasn't good enough for her.
They didn't have a hope in hell.

"Are you going to ask her to marry you? Are you
going to get her name tattooed on your butt? Are you
going to make her a playlist with a whole bunch of
love songs on it?"

Right, the kid was now starting to annoy him.
Liam lowered his glasses and when Joshua met his

eyes, scowled. "Remember that fist I planted on your jaw a few weeks back?"

Joshua rubbed the side of his face. "Yeah, you came close to breaking it."

Not even close. "Well, if you don't shut the hell up, I'll try again."

"Relax, Liam," Dutton cautioned via the tiny bud in his ear. "By the way, I've just sent an email through to your phone with regard to that DNA testing."

Liam felt his heart shrivel and his lungs collapse. This? Now? "I'm about to hand over a crap load of cash to a known criminal and you want to discuss this now?"

Dutton had the audacity to laugh. "You can do two things at once. Do you want me to give you the highlights?"

"Give me a sec." Did he? Liam knew that whatever Dutton was about to say next would change his life, on a fundamental level. He wouldn't be the same person he was right now; he might not even be, he suspected, a Christopher. Did he really want to know? Could he live with himself if he didn't find out?

No, he was done with lies, half truths and obfuscations. He needed the truth, no matter how hard it was to hear. The truth was always better than a lie…

Maybe.

No, it was. Truth *had* to win, every time. And if he wasn't a Christopher he'd deal with the ramifications—his father's will, this position on the board, in society—later.

"Tell me," Liam said, pushing the words through clenched teeth.

"Your mother is your biological mother. Your father is not."

Liam took a moment to digest his words. Hold on, what did that mean? It didn't take him long to figure it out since he knew that his parents had been married for a few years before he was born.

So that had to mean that his mother had an affair.

A bubble of hysterical laughter formed in Liam's chest. Catherine had bitched and whined and moaned and cried buckets over his father's supposed affair with Teresa. But she was the one who'd colored outside the lines and not only had an affair—she also passed off her lover's son as her husband's.

Priceless.

Liam picked up his phone and walking just far enough away from Joshua so that he couldn't hear his conversation, dialed his mother's cell.

"I do hope you've called to apologize."

Not in this lifetime.

"So, Catherine, would you like to tell me who my biological father is?" Liam asked. It was a strain to keep his voice calm and even but if he started shouting, there was a solid chance that Catherine would hang up. And he needed answers and he needed them now.

"I have no idea what you are talking about. Have you been drinking, Liam?"

Nice try, Mom. "I noticed Dad's blood type in the hospital, and I knew that people with his blood type can't produce a kid with my blood type. When I asked you about it at Dad's funeral, you said it was a typo."

Catherine's silence was hot and heavy.

"So I ordered some genetic testing done and those results came in a few minutes ago. You're my mother, but Linus wasn't my father."

"He was your father in every way that mattered—"

"Cut the crap, Mom. You had an affair—ironic, giving how much you've had to say on Dad's perceived infidelity—and pretended that I was Dad's."

"You have been drinking!"

He'd definitely inherited his stubborn gene from Catherine. "Are you denying it?"

"Until my last breath."

"Science doesn't lie, Mom, but you sure as hell do." Liam waited a beat. "I will find out."

"It's not going to change anything, Liam!" Catherine said and for the first time, Liam heard the edge of fear in her voice.

"Maybe not. Then again, it might change everything."

Liam disconnected the call and gripped the bridge of his nose. With a mother like Catherine, who only saw what she wanted to see, it was no wonder he had trust issues. Would Catherine ever tell him the truth? He doubted it. So then, how to find out who his real father was? And why did he need to?

Liam stared at the green grass beneath his leather shoes. He needed to know because he now didn't know who he was, where his real place in the world was. Was he a Christopher? What parts of him were a result of nurture and not nature? There were too many puzzle pieces of his life missing and he needed to find them, to get a clear picture of where he came from and who he was.

Until he was clear about that, he couldn't know for certain how he felt about marriage and love and…

Teresa.

He needed to know everything, to be able to show Teresa exactly who he was so that, when—if—he ever found the guts to tell her he loved her, she'd know everything. The good and the bad. It was vitally important that there was nothing between them but cold, hard truth.

Lies corroded and if he kept anything from her, whatever they had would be eaten from the inside out.

"So do you want me to dig into who your biological father might be?" Dutton asked.

Dammit, he'd forgotten about his own Fixer, listening to every word he'd uttered.

Oh, well, what was done was done. "Yeah."

"Can you give me a starting point?" Dutton asked. "Where were your folks living at the time? Please don't tell me here in Seattle."

Linus wasn't his father; Linus wasn't his father… Who was? Liam forced himself to think about Dutton's question.

"Uh… I think I remember my mom saying that I was conceived in Hawaii. My dad was building a hotel out there at the time. Before he started with tech products, he was into real estate," Liam replied. "They sold the hotel decades ago but it's still there. It's now called The Poseidon Inn."

"I'm on it. Well, I will be when we're done here."

Liam looked around, trying to act casual. "Where are you?"

"Around."

Liam walked back to the bench and sat down, resting his forearms on his thighs. He felt Joshua's eyes on his face. "You look as white as a sheet. What happened?"

Liam shook his head. "Nothing to do with you."

Joshua nodded. "Fair enough. But if you are stressed, you should talk to Teresa. She's good at listening and finding solutions."

Yeah, she was. But Liam wasn't going to burden her with his ugly past. Teresa had had too many people dumping their crap on her; he wouldn't be another one in a long line who looked to her for a solution. He was a big boy; he'd work it out for himself, his way. "There's a lot to be said for independence, Joshua. You should try it sometime."

Dutton spoke in his ear, informing him that he needed to leave if he was going to meet his contact on time. Standing, he placed a hand on Joshua's shoulder. "By the end of today your life is going to be very different. You're about to get a second chance, so don't mess it up. That being said, can you do me a favor?"

"What?"

"Wait here for me, maybe for twenty minutes, a half hour? Then we'll tackle your sister together."

Joshua nodded and Liam picked up the rucksack and walked away, trying to act like he wasn't carrying several fortunes over his shoulder.

* * *

Teresa was about to climb the walls by the time she heard a knock on her apartment door. Flying across the room, she hurdled the two suitcases she'd packed—the absolute essentials she couldn't leave behind—and yanked the door open. Her brother, looking tired but unharmed, lifted his hand in a half wave. Teresa, conscious of Liam behind him looking grim, wrapped her arms around Joshua's waist and burst into tears.

"I thought you were dead. Why didn't you answer my calls?" Teresa demanded between hiccups and sobs.

Joshua steered her backward into the room and awkwardly patted her back.

Aware that Liam had followed them into the room, she stepped away from Joshua and wiped her eyes with the balls of her hands. Teresa was so glad to see him one more time, for the last time, and she wished she could throw herself into his arms and ask him for help. But this was her mess. Well, Joshua's actually, and while she might, emphasis on the *might*, consider asking him for a loan to help her out, she couldn't ask him to risk his life.

No, her only option was to run, as soon as they could and as far as they could. Mexico? Alaska? God, it was all so overwhelming. But first, she had to get Liam to leave.

Liam nudged a suitcase with his foot. "Going somewhere?"

She didn't want to lie to him, she really didn't.

But she had already once today—and such a huge one—so the damage was done. "I'm taking Joshua on a short trip."

"No, you're bolting," Liam stated, folding his arms over his chest. "Why didn't you ask me for help instead?"

Joshua opened his mouth to speak but a hard look from Liam killed whatever he was about to say. He lifted his hands. "I'm going to give you some privacy."

Liam waited until Joshua had left the room before speaking again. "Well?"

Teresa lifted her head. "I don't need your help, Liam. I can handle whatever happens in my life."

"By running away? When did that ever help?"

It would help him to stay alive! But she couldn't tell him that! Why was he pushing her? He should be at home, cursing her name. "Why are you here? After what I said today, I never expected to see you again."

"You're a really bad liar, Teresa, and I know the truth, because I know *you*. You did not sleep with my dad and you only said that to create some distance between us. So that I would let you go."

Dammit, dammit, dammit. Teresa glanced down at her bags. "I'm going anyway."

"You're staying exactly where you are," Liam stated, his face implacable. "It's over, Teresa."

What was over? Their relationship? Yes, she already assumed as much. "I know. There's been too much craziness between us to make us work."

"That's not what I was talking about," Liam said,

pulling a small flash drive from the pocket of his suit. He handed it to her and Teresa frowned as she took the drive.

"What is this?"

"That is proof that Joshua's debts have been paid, that he is no longer in danger from any criminal element, anywhere." Liam narrowed his eyes. "But if he finds himself entangled in that world again, I will not be pleased."

Teresa heard his words but they didn't make any sense. Feeling her knees turning mushy, she sat down on the arm of her sofa and stared up at Liam. "I don't understand. How did this happen? What did you *do*?"

Liam picked up a wooden sculpture of a hummingbird on a stand and ran his thumb down its smooth back. He replaced the sculpture before jamming his hands into the pockets of his pants.

"If you'd just put your stubbornness aside and asked for my help, this could've been handled weeks ago."

"But the money…it's a lot of money. And they threatened *you*, Liam."

"The threat was an empty one and we would've figured that out together if you'd just talked to me. And it's just money, Teresa, and I have a lot of it."

But how would she ever pay him back? How would Joshua? But before she got to that, she needed to know how her life went from falling apart to…not. "Tell me everything."

Liam hesitated as if he was trying to decide where to start.

"You know I also have a guy who does things for me, someone I have on speed dial. He has connections that you and I—" Liam hesitated "—do not. He helped me arrange to pay off the debt. It's done. But as Nicolette suspected back in Napa, it was more personal than we realized, Teresa. Somebody went to a lot of effort to make your life hell."

Teresa sucked her bottom lip between her teeth. She didn't want to hear this, and she knew that Liam didn't want to tell her this part of the story. "Do you know who?"

He nodded. Liam met her eyes and in the green depths, she saw pain and mortification. "My mother."

Teresa's mouth fell open. *"What?"*

"My mother blames you for the breakup of her marriage. She refuses to accept that you didn't have an affair with Linus. She was behind the tabloid stories, the rumors, the escalation of the debt. She was also, I am mortified to admit this, behind today's threat to have me killed. She didn't mean it but she knew it would be effective."

"Your mother?" Teresa spluttered.

Liam's cheeks flushed with embarrassment. "I can't tell you how sorry I am." Liam pushed his hand through his hair and rubbed the back of his neck. "I'd completely understand if you want to press charges against her."

Teresa's brows flew up. Have his mother arrested? Was he nuts? "Could I prove anything?" she asked.

"Probably not," Liam admitted.

Teresa forced herself to think, to distance herself

from her anger. "That would create another scandal that Christopher Corporation doesn't need right now."

"I don't give a flying...fig how it affects the company." Liam pushed the words out between clenched teeth.

"Yeah, Liam, you do. And you should," Teresa said. She made a quick decision. "I'm not going to take this any further. Your mother is a sad woman and I think she is living her own type of hell."

She couldn't miss the relief that she saw in his eyes. Catherine was, after all, his mother, and although she was pampered, spoiled, narcissistic and a complete bitch, he didn't want to see her humiliated. Teresa, who'd always protected her own mother, could see that from a mile away.

Teresa stared down at her hardwood floor and allowed herself to relax, finally starting to believe that it was all over. She felt like an elephant had been lifted off her chest, like her mind had been vacuumed. Laughter, relief and joy bubbled up inside her. She wanted to throw herself into Liam's arms, express her gratitude in the most basic way she knew how... naked and horizontally.

But Liam, when she looked at him, still looked as remote as he did when he walked into her apartment. "Why do I feel like you are about to drop another bombshell?" she asked, not sure if she wanted to know.

When he just looked at her without saying anything, she shrugged. "I don't have to marry you today to save Christopher Corporation, do I?" she joked, hoping to see humor flash in his eyes.

Liam just held her eyes. "Would you? If it came down to that?"

She would. Today she'd realized that there wasn't anything she wouldn't do for him. She'd been prepared to run to save him and his reputation, to give him a life that, she'd assumed, was better without her in it. She'd given him everything and anything she could, in any way she could.

"If you wanted me to…"

Emotion as bold as a lightning strike and as fragile as a butterfly wing flashed in his eyes and in that moment, Teresa released all resistance to what she was feeling. She loved him and while she was intensely grateful that he'd saved her brother's life, her career, her home, she was not confusing gratitude with love. She loved him—intensely, passionately, forever.

What was the point of keeping her heart, that useless organ that now only thumped for him, to herself? Wasn't love—especially something so rich and wild and desperate to be free—meant to be shared?

"I love you."

She dropped the words into the quiet space between them, and she immediately felt his body tense. His eyes lightened and darkened and, for one brief moment, she thought he might reach for her, pull her into his arms, but he just stood there, his eyes locked with hers.

"I'm sorry if that's not what you want to hear but I do. I think I always have. I know I always will."

Liam ran his hand over his head, obviously agitated. "Dammit, Teresa."

Not the reaction she wanted but also not one that surprised her. She never expected Liam to drop to his knees, overcome with emotion; that wasn't his way. Besides, her love had nothing to do with his response; it just *was*.

Teresa stood up and placed her hands on his chest, looking up into his face. "You and I have had a rocky road and have dealt with things no couple should be forced to face. It's been rough and hard and tough. And that's okay. I can handle anything with you standing next to me." Teresa stroked the fabric of his shirt, feeling his hot skin beneath it, felt the *thump thump* of his heart beneath her palm. "But love, true love, grown-up love, isn't based on what you get back. It's judged by how much you give."

"I don't understand."

Teresa's smile was sad. "I know. I didn't, either. I loved my mom and protected her, loved and protected Joshua, and all I wanted was for them to love and protect me as much as I did them. I wanted something back. Maybe, initially, I wanted that from you, too.

"But now I don't expect, can't expect, you to love me just because I love you. Love is not conditional. I understand that now."

"I don't understand any of this," Liam muttered, his rigid arms still at his sides. "I've got things to work through, stuff I need to find out."

Teresa saw the confusion and misery in his eyes but knew that there was so much he wasn't telling her.

He still couldn't trust her. And she couldn't blame him. With parents like his, trust was impossible. Teresa placed her hand on his cheek. "I'll always be on your side, Liam. No matter what."

Liam covered her hand with his and closed his eyes. After a minute he told her, his voice rough with emotion, that he needed to go.

Teresa dropped her hands and blinked back her tears. "I know."

And she needed him to go before she begged him to stay.

Because love, she thought as Liam left her apartment and her life, could not be demanded.

Eleven

Teresa, dressed in yoga pants and a tank top, walked down her hallway and into her kitchen, squinting at the bright sunlight streaming in from the open windows. She loved her apartment and she was so grateful to Liam for providing her the means for her to stay in it and for, obviously, saving her brother.

While she waited for her coffee to brew, Teresa placed her elbows on the granite counter and her face in her hands. Four days had passed since Liam handed her the flash drive and their freedom and she and Joshua had spent that time getting used to the idea that they were free.

Since she'd repaid The Fixer by organizing Brooks's wedding, Teresa was also free of him. Corinne was fielding a bunch of queries for her to organize events and had already delegated some of the smaller, less high-profile events to her staff. Corinne had also declared that Teresa needed a few days off so, not having the energy to argue, Teresa opted to stay home. But she'd had enough of doing nothing except missing Liam.

Thinking about Liam.

Needing Liam.

Teresa tried to ignore the knife in her heart, the barbed wire wrapped around her stomach. She should go back to work; she wanted her life to go back to normal, but most of all, she wanted to go back to Liam.

Teresa heard her front door opening and walked through to her living room, frowning. Joshua slept late as often as he could and frequently didn't surface until around noon. God, she needed to do something about her brother and soon.

She loved him but she couldn't live with him.

Joshua walked into the living room, his body sweaty. What was going on? Joshua didn't exercise. Ever.

"Are you feeling okay?" she asked.

Joshua ran a hand towel over his glistening face. "Fine, why?"

"It's not even seven thirty and you've been exercising. What's up with that?"

Joshua rubbed his head with his towel and Teresa thought she heard something about Liam and boxing. Yanking his towel away, she glared at him. "Say that again?"

"Liam told me that I had to be at his gym at six

this morning," Joshua told her, heading in the direction of the kitchen. Teresa followed him, trying to make sense of his words. Joshua pulled a bottle of water from the fridge and Teresa grabbed the edge of his T-shirt as he tried to edge past her to go to his room. "Hold on there, Josh. You went to the gym with Liam?"

"Yep."

"Why?"

"Because he told me I had to. I started two days ago," Joshua replied, holding her intense stare. Okay, so that was new. It had been ages since Joshua had managed to maintain eye contact.

"And why are you listening to Liam?"

Joshua lifted a thin shoulder. "Because I owe him."

Teresa started to protest but Joshua slapped his hand over her mouth. His sweaty, recently-been-in-a-glove hand. Yuck. Teresa shuddered and slapped it away. She pointed to a bar stool next to the counter. "Sit. And explain."

"I can never repay Liam the seven mil, I know that," Joshua said.

"I'll repay him when I sell the shares back to him."

Joshua smiled. "He said you'd say that and he said to remind you that he doesn't want your money." Joshua took another long pull of water before carefully placing his bottle on the counter. "Besides, the money has nothing to do with you."

Teresa frowned at him. "Maybe so but you don't have the money to repay Liam."

"I know that. So does Liam," Joshua said, sounding irritated. "But it doesn't change the fact that it's my problem, not yours."

Okay, technically true but she'd looked after Joshua all his life.

"Liam says it's time that I act my age, that I take responsibility for my actions." Joshua lifted his chin and Teresa saw her own stubbornness in his eyes. "I'm working it out with him."

Oh. *Ohhhh*. She narrowed her eyes, not pleased. What was Liam up to? She loved the man but she'd still go to war with him over Josh. He was still her baby brother.

"Liam expects me at the gym four mornings a week," Joshua replied. "I'm also starting work at Christopher Corporation next week Monday. And I'm going to school at night." Teresa opened her mouth to ask how he was going to pay for school but Joshua beat her to it. "Apparently, Christopher Corporation has a few interns who work shorter hours for a smaller salary and study part-time."

So, wow. "What are you going to study?"

Joshua ducked his head. "I'm really interested in computers. Maybe software engineering?"

"That sounds great," Teresa said, still needing to know more. "How long do you have to work for Liam?"

"He didn't say. He just wants me to give it a decent shot. He says that he believes that I can do anything I want to, if I started to trust myself and if I made decent decisions."

Teresa placed a hand on her heart, thinking it

might beat out of her chest. Man, Liam was such a good man. A good man who was keeping his distance. She could just slap him. Why were they being miserable apart when they could be happy together?

"I'm proud of you, Josh. I think you're going to be just fine," Teresa said, patting his hand. She wanted to hug him but she'd do that after he'd showered.

Joshua rocked the bottle of water from side to side. "You both have the same look in your eyes. Both of you are so damn unhappy but trying to be strong."

Well, that was what adults did. "I'm glad you get to spend time with Liam, Josh. He's a really good man."

"A good guy with a hell of a right hook," Joshua said, rubbing his jaw. "Did he tell you that his mom paid some guys to drug me, and that they suggested that I crash that party and insult those people?"

Not exactly but she'd figured that was what happened. "Catherine is convinced that I slept with Liam's dad and she wanted to punish me."

"She's nutso."

Teresa agreed with him. "Liam explained everything to me. His mother is a loon, his father isn't his father and that's why he's off to Oahu this morning," Joshua said.

What?

"Whoa, back up. What did you say?"

"Liam flew to Oahu."

"No! What do you mean that his father isn't his father?"

Joshua looked guilty. "I don't know if I should've mentioned that. It wasn't like he *told* me that."

She was going to wrap her hands around his throat and squeeze the information out of him. "Tell me exactly what he said, Joshua David."

Josh winced when she used his full name. Good, she was not playing around. "Yesterday I told Liam that I was heading straight home but I changed my mind and headed to the showers. I think Liam thought they were alone–"

"Who is *they*?" Teresa demanded.

"Oh, his friend Matt joined us for a workout."

"Go on."

"I only got bits and pieces of what he was saying. He mentioned DNA testing and that someone called Dutton had tracked down his real dad. And that he was still in Hawaii." Josh pushed his wet hair off his forehead. "Then today Liam tells me that he's flying his plane to Oahu, that he has some business there to see to. It wasn't difficult to add two and two together."

Teresa stood up, needing to pace the small area between the living room and the kitchen island. Typical Liam, determined to do everything by himself. When would he realize that she was on his side? That they were stronger together than they were apart? She'd tried to give him space, to give him time to reach the conclusion she had but she was running out of patience.

Stopping abruptly, she sent Joshua a hard look. "Do you know where he was going in Oahu?"

Joshua shook his head. "Nope. Why, are you thinking of joining him?"

Teresa slapped her hands on her hips and narrowed

her eyes. "I don't care if you think it's a bad idea. I'm going anyway."

Joshua shook his head. "I think it's a great idea. You love him and he, I'm convinced, loves you. It's stupid to be apart. You might run out of time."

Just like their parents had. Teresa nodded. She and Joshua both understood how important it was to live in the moment, yet she was here and Liam was not. She was over it.

"How are you going to find him?" Joshua asked, genuinely curious. "Oahu is a big island."

Happy to have something to do, a direction to follow, Teresa flashed him a grin. "Watch and learn, young one." Picking up her phone, she punched in the number and put the device on loudspeaker.

"Liam Christopher's office."

After greeting Duncan, Teresa demanded to know where Liam was.

Duncan, being the professional he was, refused to tell her. "I'm sure if Liam wanted you to know his whereabouts, he would've told you himself, Teresa."

"Duncan, don't make me turn mean." Teresa kept her tone pleasant.

"Threats won't work on me but feel free to try your luck," Duncan said, a hint of laughter in his voice.

Teresa winked at Joshua. "Really? Tell me, Duncan, how much of a pain in the ass is Catherine Christopher?"

"Huge. Massive. Freakin' ginormous."

"All that and she's only Liam's mother."

"And what is that supposed to mean?" Duncan asked, all humor now gone.

"I fully intend to be Liam's wife and I can either be utterly wonderful or so obnoxious you'll think Catherine is a pussycat. You telling me exactly where Liam is will help me make that decision."

"You're too nice to be a bitch."

"But do you want to take that chance?"

Duncan replied something inaudible and muttered out an address. Teresa grabbed a pen from the container and wrote the name of the hotel on her hand. "Thanks, Duncan."

"Sure. It'll be your fault if he fires me," Duncan said.

"Duncan, if he fires you, I'll hire you. Deal?"

"At a ten percent salary increase and an extra week vacation time," Duncan stated, as quick as ever.

She could never afford Duncan. He was too highly paid for her company but it was a moot point because Liam would never let Duncan go. Ever.

She didn't think.

"Thanks. I owe you," Teresa told him before disconnecting the call. She looked at Josh and allowed him to see her sudden uncertainty. "Am I doing the right thing?"

"Are you asking me?" Josh clarified and when she nodded, he shrugged. "I don't have a clue but at least you're trying. That's got to count for something."

Man, she sure hoped so.

Nic wound her arms around her knees and watched as the Caribbean sky turned from blue to pink as the super-hot day faded away. She looked down at her arms, thinking that she couldn't remember when last she looked so tan, how long it had been since she'd had a proper vacation. When last had she felt so utterly relaxed?

That would be…never.

But time was running away from them and tomorrow they would be on an Abbingdon jet and heading back to Seattle and real life. Except that she had no idea what her real life entailed. Over the past week, she and Brooks had laughed and loved and talked but they'd both avoided talking about the future. It was as if they were both trying to circumvent what came next, living utterly and absolutely in the moment. But Nic needed to know where she was going to sleep tomorrow night, whether she'd be in her own bed or his. She was legally married to him but their marriage was, despite spending every moment together lately, one of convenience. They were both getting something they needed from the deal and that was all that had been promised.

She was such a fool for wanting more, for wanting everything. She'd been raised by a tough cookie grandmother who refused to feed her a diet of princess and happily-ever-after stories. Life is what you make it, she'd said. It's hard and tough and cold and there isn't a prince out there who is going to hand you a shoe or awaken you from a deep sleep with a kiss.

You buy your own damn shoes and don't put yourself in a position where you require rescuing.

Except that she did, sort of, have a prince and he did own jets and luxury vacation houses with private beaches.

But everything good comes to an end, Nic. You know this. Do not expect anything from Brooks but his contacts to get your documentary flighted because if you do, you will get your heart broken.

You don't need him; you will be fine on your own. Always have been, always will be.

Nic felt the air move and looked up to see Brooks dropping to the sand next to her, stretching out long legs and digging his heels into the sand. He dumped a silver ice bucket containing a bottle of Moët between them and she saw the two flutes in his other hand.

Champagne on the beach. It was, Nic supposed, the perfect way to end a perfect week.

Brooks didn't say anything as he popped the cork and poured the pale liquid into her glass. Nic waited for him to pour champagne into his glass before clinking hers against his. "Thank you."

Brooks took a sip of champagne. "For what?"

"The best week of my life. I've loved every second," Nic said. She sipped and smiled when the champagne bubbles popped on the back of her tongue. That was what happened to her skin when Brooks kissed her, well, anywhere.

"I love it here," Brooks admitted. "I try to come as often as I can. Which isn't, I admit, nearly often enough."

Nic felt the hot flash of jealously. Who else had he brought here and had he loved those women in the same bed, in the shower, in the damned Jacuzzi? *Ack.*

"This has always been my bolt-hole, the place I

come to be alone. You're the first person I've brought here."

"Oh."

Brooks nudged her with his shoulder. "I saw that streak of jealousy, Mrs. Abbingdon."

That title sounded weird but right. So damn right.

"Admit it. You were jealous thinking of me sharing this space with someone else."

Play it cool, Nic. Shrug his comment away. He was just teasing her. She wanted to utter something pithy, something horribly sophisticated but she couldn't form the words. So she went for the truth. "Yeah, I was, am, jealous."

Brooks was quiet for a minute and when Nic looked at him, she saw something in his eyes that made her heart stumble and the champagne-flavored moisture in her mouth disappear. "What?" she asked.

"The thought of you being anywhere, with any other man, makes my head want to explode. Hell, the thought of you, being with anyone else, ever, makes my skin crawl."

What was he trying to say? Nic pulled her finger through the sand. When she realized that she'd drawn a heart, she hastily swiped her palm across the sand. The sky was now shot with tangerine flames but all Nic's attention was on Brooks. "What happens tomorrow?"

"We go back to Seattle."

Nic sent him a don't-be-obtuse look. "I mean with us. We discussed getting married and what we wanted out of it but we didn't discuss how we were going to live in this arrangement."

"Yeah, it did get a bit mad," Brooks admitted, scratching his left shoulder with his right hand. Nic watched his muscles ripple and told herself to concentrate. This was not a good time to get distracted; who knew what she might find herself agreeing to next?

"What do you want to do, Nic? We can live together or apart. It's up to you."

"If we lived together, would we be living together? I mean, sleeping together?"

"Damn straight," Brooks answered in his typical, no-nonsense way. "There is no way I could live in the same house as you and have you sleeping in another bed."

"Oh." Nic waved at the sunset. "I thought that you might want to leave this all here?"

"Why would you think that?" Brooks asked, his voice tender.

"Because this is pretend, Brooks. This is warm seas and good food, no worries, no stress. This is a vacation thing. It's not real life. You haven't lived with me when I have PMS, when I'm on a deadline, when I'm so tired I get super-bitchy."

"And you haven't lived with me when I've had a bad day or am arguing with my grandfather or I've lost a deal. I understand that this isn't real life. Real life is messy and hard and gritty and generally crazy."

"And you still want me in yours?"

Brooks leaned sideways and placed a kiss on her temple. "Yeah."

Brooks wrapped a strong arm around her shoulder and Nic leaned into him, immediately finding that super-comfortable spot to rest her head.

"Nic?"

"Mmm?"

"I'm not telling you that I love you—" Nic pulled away and looked up into his masculine face. In the fading light his eyes turned lighter and brighter. But it was his words that transfixed her, that kept all her attention on his beautifully masculine face "—but I'm not telling you that I don't, either. I like you. I like you more than a lot. More than any woman I've ever known. I want—"

Brooks pulled a face and Nic was charmed by the sudden redness in his cheeks. "I want you in my bed, for you to be there when I come home or to be waiting for you to come home if you are late. I want to share showers and breakfasts and my body with you. But—"

Oh, God, here it came, the big *but*.

"But a part of me also wants you to go back to your place so that I can pick you up for a date. I want to take it slow so that I can seduce the hell out of my wife. I want to take you to Paris for the weekend or skiing in Tahoe. I want it all and I want it all right now."

Nic released the air she was holding, feeling like every part of her was smiling. Turning, she swung her leg over Brooks's thigh and when she faced him, wound her arms around his neck. She pressed her forehead against his and crossed her eyes, making him laugh.

"Well, Mr. Abbingdon, then I have a proposal for you. I'll live with you over weekends and I'll date you during the week." She kissed the tip of his nose before pulling back. "And if you're very, very lucky, and if you play your cards right, I might, sometime in the future, agree to marry you."

The corners of Brooks's sexy mouth lifted. "Let me think about that, Mrs. Abbingdon. It's a big step. A lot of factors should be considered." He brushed his mouth across hers, lifting his lips to murmur a "Hell, yes" against her lips.

"Yes to what, Brooks?"

"Everything, darling. For the rest of our lives."

Twelve

Liam sat down at a table situated on the balcony of The Veranda, the trendy meeting place just off the lobby of the luxurious Kahala Hotel. He glanced over the beach, pool and dolphin lagoon and wished Teresa was here, knowing she'd get a kick out of this luxury hotel located just a few minutes from the famous Waikiki Beach.

Liam ordered a Manhattan from a waiter and wiped his hand on his thigh. He couldn't remember when last he'd been this nervous. This was nerves on a whole new level. Damn, he really wanted Teresa here. Somehow, she had a way of calming him, of silently reminding him that it was okay, that he was okay. That he mattered…

Liam thanked the waiter for his drink and picked

up the brown envelope he'd placed on the table earlier. He'd spent hours looking at the photographs Dutton sent him, had read his report a dozen times, maybe more. His father was John Hamilton. He'd been born and raised on the island, and had three college-aged daughters. Liam paused, thinking that he had three sisters. He'd always wanted a sibling—someone to help share the burden of his mother's cloying love, protectiveness and general craziness. Now he had three. Well, intellectually he had three; he didn't know if he'd ever get to meet them.

He had to meet his father first, and John Hamilton had agreed to meet him here, at The Veranda, in, Liam glanced at his watch, three minutes.

Liam lifted his hand and grimaced at his trembling fingers. This was big, this was huge, this might all blow up in his face.

What did he want from John? What did he need? Would they keep in touch or would this one meeting be it? Would he meet his wife or would he want to keep Liam separate from his real family? Would he want money? Was he only meeting with Liam because he was loaded? God, maybe this wasn't such a great idea…maybe he should go.

"You're Liam."

Showtime. Liam hauled in a deep breath and stood up, giving his hands one last swipe. He turned slowly and saw himself, plus thirty years. Gray-flecked dark hair, lined eyes and the same long nose. Liam stared at his father for a minute and eventually lifted his hand for a handshake. John gripped his hand and

Liam thought, just for a fraction of a second, that he wanted to pull him in and hug him. But grown men seldom did that, and Christophers never.

Liam gestured for John to sit and they stared at each other. John was the first to break the awkward silence. He rubbed his chin as he propped his foot on his opposite knee. "I never expected to hear from you."

Liam reached for his Manhattan and then realized that John probably needed something to drink, as well. He called over a waiter.

"I think this conversation calls for some liquid courage," Liam said as the waiter approached him. "What would you like?"

"Whatever you are having."

When the waiter left, Liam spoke. "Did you know about me?"

"Yeah. Initially, your mother refused to admit it but I knew that you were mine. The dates worked." John dropped his knee and leaned forward. "First off, you need to know that I am not proud of myself. She was married and she should've been firmly off-limits but damn, she was entrancing."

"How did you meet?" Liam asked.

"Linus was building a hotel here and I was working for the landscaper who was building the gardens. Your mother loved horticulture and your father gave her free reign to do whatever she wanted in the grounds. God, she changed her mind a million times and it made us crazy. Eventually, the boss couldn't deal with her and handed the project over to me. One thing led to another…"

"How long were you together?"

"Nearly a year. Linus wasn't always around. He was establishing the tech arm of your company at that point and he was consumed by that. Catherine was about five months pregnant when he sold the hotel and she left the island."

"Did you want her to stay?"

John winced. "Honestly? Probably not. But I sure as hell wanted you. But Linus was her husband. He could give her, and you, everything I couldn't. Then."

"Then?"

John's smile held a hint of pride along with sadness. "If she'd just been prepared to hang tough for a few years, I could've given her most of what Linus could. I opened my own landscaping business and then a garden supply store. Within five years I had ten. Now I have a lot more."

Liam's agile mind connected the dots. "You're the Hamilton of Hamilton's Home and Garden Stores?"

John nodded. "I handed the day-to-day running of the company over to a group of young, sharp business people and I spend my days surfing or in my garden. Or bugging my wife." John smiled. "I'm keeping the business for a couple of years to see if any of my kids want to run it but none of my girls have shown any interest. Do you want it?"

Liam jerked back, shocked. "You can't give it to me!"

John cocked his head. "Why not? You're my kid, too."

Wait, this was madness. "You don't know me, John."

John picked up the rucksack he'd walked in with and pulled three bulging files from the bag. He put them on the table and slapped the top cover. "Part of the deal with your mom to keep my mouth shut about you was that she send me all your school records, achievements and a monthly report. There's thirty-plus years of info on you in there, most of which you've probably forgotten. I might not have raised you but I know you."

Liam rubbed the back of his neck as he flipped open the cover of the top file. His Apgar scores jumped out at him, as well as a picture of him a few minutes old, looking like a pissed-off monkey. Liam flipped through the file, reports, his first karate belt, a spelling bee he entered. More photos. John wasn't lying; this was his life, in three files.

"Why didn't you contact me when I was older?" Liam quietly asked.

"Catherine promised to tell you who your real father was when you turned eighteen. We agreed that it would be your choice as to whether you reached out. You didn't so I assumed that you weren't interested in meeting me," John said and Liam heard the hurt in his voice.

"Yeah, my mother isn't great at keeping her word," Liam replied. "I only recently figured out that someone with my blood group couldn't be a product of their combined DNA." Liam blew air over his lips. "My mother is a piece of work."

John nodded. "Am I allowed to say, as respectfully as possible, that I know that I dodged a bullet? Heidi, my wife, who knows about you by the way, and I have been married for twenty-six years and we're ridiculously happy."

Liam's mouth curved up. "That's wonderful. And encouraging."

John tapped his finger against his tumbler. He smiled knowingly. "Who is she?"

Liam thought about lying but decided he didn't have the energy. "Teresa St. Claire. We've had this crazy, crazy relationship, thanks in part to my mother's interference and machinations. It's been…complicated."

John frowned and clicked his fingers, something Liam realized that he also did when he was thinking. "Teresa St. Claire. Didn't she inherit a large portion of your father's shares of Christopher Corporation?"

"Twenty-five percent and how do you know that?" Liam asked, surprised.

John nodded to the folders. "When you turned eighteen your mother cut off my supply of Liam-related information. I hired a PI to keep me informed." Liam wanted to think that was creepy but he just felt…treasured. Cherished. Like he had a father who really, really cared about him.

"St. Claire, damn, that name sounds familiar."

Liam frowned. "Teresa's dad briefly worked for my dad but that was before I was born."

"That's it! I remember Catherine talking about him ad infinitum."

Liam leaned forward, immediately interested. "Do you remember those conversations?"

John gave it some thought. "I remember her being in a snit, for days, because Linus wanted to pay him a whack of cash for something—a formula?—and Catherine objected because Linus had what he needed from St. Claire already. I remember arguing about who owned the rights to intellectual property, the individual or the company."

Holy, holy smokes. Around the time he was born, his dad had launched the tech division of Christopher Corporation, the division that eventually became the heart of the company. And Nigel St. Claire must have developed the code for their biggest selling product, a software program that revolutionized web security. The software that made the Christophers rich beyond belief.

"What else do you remember about him?"

"St. Claire? Mmm, let me think. He left the country for some reason and I think that one or both of your parents made it difficult for the guy to come back to the States. Something about knowing someone in Immigration and St. Claire's expired visa, I think. Catherine mentioned something about him not being able to sue them if he was out of the country."

Liam gripped the edges of his nose, trying to control his anger. His parents kept Nigel from his kids. Man, his image of his parents was tarnishing minute by minute. But his father—Linus—obviously felt guilty about it because he'd tried to make restitution to Nigel's family by leaving Teresa the shares.

Crap, what a tangled, complicated mess.

When he told Teresa why her dad didn't come

home, why he couldn't come home for so long, she was going to flip. Catherine had already tried to mess with her life, to ruin her reputation and torch her business, but Teresa had handled that. But Catherine, or Linus, or both, had conspired to keep her father from returning to the States. That she wouldn't forgive. Everybody had issues with their partner's families but this was beyond what was acceptable.

He'd have to tell her but he knew that it would be the mortal blow that would fracture their already fragile relationship. How would she be able to live with and love the man whose family destroyed hers?

"Liam, look at me."

Liam forced his eyes up, surprised at the forceful note in John's voice, the determination in his eyes.

"What your parents did does not reflect on you. You are only responsible for the things you do and the things you say. You are your own man."

"But I'm dealing with the consequences of their actions," Liam pointed out.

John grimaced. "For that I am sorry. I'm also sorry I didn't fight harder for you. I genuinely believed that they could give you what I couldn't."

Liam felt a surge of anger, for the reserved, scared, frequently overwhelmed kid he'd been. "Yeah, John, I had the latest toys and the brand-name clothing and the holidays in exotic places. But you know what I didn't have? I didn't have a father who came to my sports matches or who spent any time throwing a ball. Praise was given when I achieved an A and withdrawn when I messed up. I handed my mother tissues when she cried over something my father would or wouldn't do and I handed him the whiskey bottle when he bitched about her."

Liam stood up, unable to deal with any more, feeling emotionally shattered. "But you know, I had the toys and the clothes and the holidays."

John scrambled to his feet and placed his hand on Liam's arm. "Don't rush off, Liam. Let's talk."

Liam stared at a point behind his shoulder, not seeing the gold and pink sunset, the soft sea. He stepped back and shook his head. "I can't. Not anymore."

Liam picked up his brown envelope, sent another look at the files and shook his head. He needed to go; he couldn't take any more and he definitely needed to leave. And God, he needed another drink. Or ten.

"Am I going to see you again?" John asked, his green eyes worried.

"I don't know, John," Liam replied, walking away. All he knew for sure is that he needed some quiet, some peace and to stop thinking.

But more than anything he needed Teresa.

Teresa ran her hand over her hip and looked down at the satin material below her hand. The designer dress, the one she last wore at Hunter and Jenna's wedding, was the purest shade of daffodil yellow and the color, along with its deep neckline, body-skimming shape and shortish skirt was a weapon set to stun. She knew that the yellow brought out the blue of her eyes and she'd deliberately applied more eyeshadow than normal, creating a deep and sexy smoky eye effect. She'd contoured her cheekbones and swiped a thin layer of pink gloss over her lips. Under her dress she only wore ludicrously expensive French perfume.

She intended to seduce the hell out of Liam Christopher.

She wanted him cross-eyed and naked. And, preferably, so discombobulated that he'd drop his guard and tell her how much he loved her and how he couldn't live without her. She wanted him to tell her about meeting his father, and how he felt about the past.

Though, in all honesty, if she just got him to forget to ask how she knew he was in Hawaii, she'd take that as a minor win.

Taking a breath, Teresa knocked on the door to the presidential suite and when he didn't answer, knocked again. If he wasn't in his suite, she had no idea how to find him. And she didn't have a place to go since she hadn't reserved a hotel room. She supposed she could go and hang out in the bar and try again later. But what if Liam had left and was on his way back to Seattle?

No, she refused to accept that she'd wasted the flight and this dress. Teresa banged on the door again and nearly wept when she heard male footsteps on the other side of the door.

"I didn't order room service—" Liam said as he opened the door. Teresa had planned on saying something sexy like "Let's misbehave" but her words dried on her tongue. A wet Liam, wearing just a white towel around his hips, glowered down at her, acres and acres of tanned skin just waiting to be touched. His eyes were wide with shock and he placed a hand on the door frame as if to steady himself.

"Teresa? You're here?"

"I'm here," Teresa said, ducking under his arm. Inside the suite, she sucked in a breath at the luxury furnishings—damn, she always forgot how rich Liam was—before turning around to see Liam stalking toward her.

"Aren't you going to ask me why I'm here?" Teresa asked, then did a mental facepalm. She didn't want him asking questions, not yet anyway.

Later, when she'd loved him so thoroughly and fried his brain, she'd tell him that their being apart was ridiculous and that they were supposed to be together. She'd ask him about his dad…

"I don't give a rat's ass why you're here. I was in the shower, wishing you were with me," Liam growled. He reached her and cupped her face, his fingers pushing into her hair, which she'd left to flow down her shoulders. Liam picked up a strand and ran it through his fingers. "I always forget how long it is. How silky."

Teresa placed her hands on his waist and drew circles on his bare skin with her thumbs. She turned her mouth to kiss his palm and kept her eyes connected with him. "And just what were you doing in the shower while you were thinking of me?"

"You know what I was doing," Liam muttered, taking her hand and placing it on his hard cock. He felt hard and full and desperate beneath her hand and Teresa released a low hum of approval. Liam placed his forehead against hers and sighed. "You're really here."

Teresa briefly wondered why he kept saying that, why he was acting like having her here was like a dream he expected to be jerked from. Teresa's eyes connected with his and saw misery and confusion and a whole bunch of regret. Dammit. Needing to chase his ghosts away, Teresa linked her arms around his neck and stood on her tiptoes—her nude high heels, as sexy as they were, still didn't give her the height she needed—and rested her mouth against his. Speaking softly, she whispered the words against his lips. "If you need me, Liam, take me."

"You might regret saying that," Liam muttered as his hand drifted over her ass.

"I'll never regret anything to do with you," Teresa told him.

Liam released a short, harsh laugh but before she could comment on his cynicism, he covered her mouth with his and twisted his tongue around hers. His strong arms pulled her into him and her breasts pushed into hard chest, instantly dampening her dress from a combination of heat and lust and shower droplets.

Liam held her head so that he could possess her mouth, pulling her bottom lip between his teeth. As if he couldn't get enough, he yanked his mouth away to nibble her jaw, to that sexy place where her jawbone met her ear and then down the cord of her neck. Teresa felt her eyes cross and she grabbed his chin, wanting more of his mouth, his lips, his tongue. Liam fed her what she wanted, what she craved: long, hot, drugging, push-reality-away kisses.

Conscious of her swimming head, Teresa whimpered when he pulled away from her to run a finger down the deep vee of her neckline.

"Love this dress but it would be so much better on the floor."

The thought—that the dress was too expensive and too precious to end up on any floor—whispered past her and evaporated when Liam turned her around and placed his fingers on the zipper. She felt his breath on her back following the zip down her body and shuddered when his mouth kissed her lower spine. She was already wet and pulsing. It wouldn't take much for her to come…

Liam straightened, brushed the dress from her shoulders and Teresa heard his appreciative gasp when he realized that she was come-take-me-baby naked beneath the dress.

"I'm liking that dress better and better," Liam said, his hand coming across her torso to cup her breast. He lightly pinched her nipple and Teresa bucked, more from pleasure than pain.

"You are so beautiful. You're everything I want."

Liam murmured in her ear as he lifted her hair to kiss the back of her neck. She felt his mouth moving down her spine again, his hands sliding over her stomach, over her thin patch of hair and down the front of her thighs. Needing him, needing more, Teresa spun around.

Liam, now on his knees, looked up at her. "Perfect. You're exactly where I wanted you."

Teresa stared down at his dark head as he spread her folds and gently kissed her mound. Teresa felt her legs wobble and locked her knees, sighing when Liam's clever fingers slipped into her heat. Teresa pushed her fingers into his hair, tugging him closer, silently demanding more. When Teresa didn't think she could take his teasing any longer, Liam licked her, his hot tongue creating a blazing trail. A finger, then another, slid inside her and Teresa whipped her head from side to side. It was too much; she'd wanted to love him like this; she'd wanted to drive him crazy, take him outside himself, but she was on the receiving end.

She wasn't strong enough to ask him to stop.

Liam's tongue flicked her clit, his fingers twisted inside her and Teresa felt herself spinning away, a hot, whirling dervish of pure sensation. Teresa peaked, sank, peaked again and as she was falling back, Liam grabbed her ass, boosted her up his body and entered her with one long, hard stroke. She was so wet, so turned on, that her eyes rolled back in her head and her inner muscles clenched, wanting more. Wanting it all.

Again.

Liam moved her dead weight as if she were a piece of lint and sank down onto the closest chair. Teresa used her knees to lift herself up so that she just had his tip inside her before sliding back down again. Opening her eyes, she looked into his foggy gaze and thought that this was love. This perfect jumble of sensations—lust, excitement, passion, trust—this was love.

Love was also waking up with him every morning, giving him a child, making him feel like he was the most important part of her day, that he was her world.

Because he was. Tears filled her eyes and rolled down her cheeks and Liam brushed them away with his fingers. "Teresa? What's wrong?"

Teresa just shook her head.

"Do you want to stop?"

Teresa shook her head and pushed down on him, making him groan. Her man…only Liam would offer to stop at the sight of her tears, even though he was so deep inside her she wasn't sure where he ended and she began, that he was trembling as he tried to keep control.

She loved him. Up until that moment, she never understood how much, but now she could feel it in every cell, every heartbeat, every look and stroke and kiss.

"Let go, Liam," she murmured, gently touching his face, running her thumb along his jawline. "Let go and take me with you."

Liam launched himself upward and using his core muscles picked her up and whipped her off the chair. The floor was the closest horizontal surface and he laid her on the Persian carpet, picked up her one leg and slammed into her.

"Not going to be able to wait."

Teresa felt that delicious curling sensation deep

within her and knew that she was a heartbeat behind him. She felt Liam tense, heard his guttural moan and then his hand was between them and his thumb flicked her bead and her soul shattered.

This, this was love and it was wonderful.

So, in fact, were her multiple, earth-shattering orgasms.

Liam ran his hand down Teresa's spine, feeling every bump and dip. Her skin was utterly flawless except for three freckles perfectly placed under her right shoulder blade. Maybe there were more on her body; he'd have to check. But not, unfortunately, now. They needed to talk.

He didn't want to but he was an adult and adults did what they needed to do. Adults like his parents did what they wanted to do and damn the consequences. He would not be following in their footsteps. But Linus and Catherine weren't his only parents; he also had John, whose shoes, from the little he knew of him, might be worth stepping into.

Or maybe he could just wear his own. Create his own path, strike out on his own, be exactly the person he was. The thought was liberating. And thrilling. But would he be walking that path alone? Teresa had said she'd loved him but, after hearing about the role his family played in her father's life, would she still?

There was only one way to find out.

As if she'd heard his silent plea for her attention, Teresa rolled over and sent him a soft smile. "We made love for most of the night so I suppose I must pay the piper."

"What do you mean?"

"We need to talk, Teresa."

They, very unfortunately, did. Teresa sat up and pulled the sheet up, covering her beautiful breasts, a crime beyond comprehension. Then again, there was no way he could concentrate on any conversation while she was naked.

Hell, even knowing she was naked under the bedclothes was messing with his head.

"Let's order some coffee and take it onto the balcony," Liam suggested, rolling out of bed. He yanked on a pair of boxer shorts he'd left on the chair and fished in the chest of drawers for a T-shirt, which he tossed her way. Leaving the bedroom, he walked into the lounge, knowing that if he stayed, they'd be making love again. The longer she stayed, the harder it would be for him to watch her walk away.

And she'd walk away. That was a given.

Liam ordered coffee from his personal concierge and opened the floor-to-ceiling doors that led onto the private balcony. He gripped the railing and sighed when Teresa wound her arms around his waist and buried her face in the hollow of his spine. She felt so tiny against him, so feminine.

"Please don't fire Duncan for telling me where you are."

Liam frowned and turned around. He almost laughed at Teresa's face, her expression a perfect combination of guilt and mischief. "I threatened the hell out of him if he didn't tell me."

Okay, this was going to be good. Duncan was not a pushover and he knew the rules. "Okay. What did you threaten him with?"

Teresa drew patterns on the tiles with her big toe. "Your mother. Well, not precisely your mother." She blushed, which he found adorable. "I told him that if he didn't tell me I would make his life a living hell, acting ten times worse than Catherine, after we were married."

His heart bounced at the thought of marriage. "I should fire him," Liam teased, happy to have a moment of levity before the storm crashed over them. "My privacy is sacrosanct."

"But if you fire him then I have to hire him and give him a ten percent raise. I can't afford him!" Teresa wailed.

Liam threw his head back and laughed. Nobody but Teresa could amuse him and make him as happy and horny as she did. What if he didn't tell her about her dad? What if he took this moment, told her he loved her and took every other moment from here on out to be happy? It was so damn tempting but Liam knew that a relationship could not be built on a foundation of lies.

It wasn't really a lie but an omission…

And he was splitting hairs. His self-respect and his immense respect for her, for everything she'd done for her family, demanded that she know the truth.

Liam heard the door to the suite open and he

pushed Teresa behind him, hiding her with his bulk as the concierge pushed a trolley laden with a silver coffeepot, bone china cups and a pile of fresh-baked pastries and a bowl of refreshing fruit salad. Coffee, thank God.

Once the concierge left, Teresa immediately picked up a croissant and lifted it to her nose. "Heavenly."

Liam poured coffee while Teresa pulled small chunks from the croissant and lifted them to her mouth. Liam handed her a cup of coffee and gestured for her to take a seat on the lounger.

Sitting opposite her, he cradled his cup in his hand and thought that her eyes were the exact color of the Pacific Ocean below them.

"I met my dad yesterday, my biological father."

Teresa immediately put her croissant on a plate and placed her cup on the table between them. She crossed her legs and leaned forward, every strand of her DNA focused on him as he explained the recent events.

"And?" she asked. "What was your biological father like?"

Liam shrugged. "He was…nice. He looks like me or I look like him."

"Was he happy to meet you? Did he know about you? Why didn't he contact you?"

Liam explained the circumstances of Catherine's infidelity, and John's reasoning around letting him be raised as a Christopher. Her eyes welled up when he mentioned the scrapbooks. His Teresa, under her capable attitude, had a very tender heart.

"Are you going to meet him again?" Teresa asked.

Liam lifted both shoulders to his ears. "I don't know. I left in a mood."

Teresa's eyes sharpened and the fingers clasping her knee tightened. "A mood?"

"I was pissed off."

"Because he didn't try to find you? Because your sisters had what sounded to be a great childhood and you didn't? Because of your mother's I-can-judge-but-don't-judge-me view of life?"

All of those, he supposed. "I was most pissed off about what I heard about your dad."

"My dad? How did the subject of *my* father come up?" Teresa asked, genuinely confused.

Liam sat his cup down and rested his forearms on his knees. "John, my biological dad, filled in a missing puzzle piece, something I couldn't work out."

"Which is?"

"The real reason Linus left those shares to you," Liam said. Oh, her shoulders were already tensing, her mouth tightening. They were wandering into stormy weather here.

Liam lifted his hand. "Just hear me out, please?"

"I thought we'd moved past this," Teresa muttered.

"Look, as much as Linus liked you, and I do believe he liked you and appreciated your fine mind, he was not the type of man who would leave his shares, worth millions, to someone outside the family, no matter how fond he was of that person. He lived for Christopher Corporation. And if you didn't sleep with him—" Teresa growled and Liam ignored the sound, pushing on "—and I believe that you didn't, then why would he bequeath you those shares?"

Teresa threw up her hands, obviously irritated. "I don't know, Liam. If I knew, I'd tell you."

"But I *do* know, Teresa."

Teresa frowned, stared at him, and her frown deepened. "Okay, you know. So are you going to share?"

Liam felt like a free diver, standing on a ninety-foot cliff, unsure whether there were rocks below in the water or not. He had no option but to dive.

"Your father, Nigel, worked for my father when he was an intern. He developed code for super-secure web-based encryption and that discovery catapulted our company into the big leagues. From there we were able to hire some of the best minds in the world and we have diversified into artificial intelligence. But that code, that was how we got our start."

Liam pulled on his earlobe. "Your father created that code, and the policy at the time was that any developments made at Christopher Corporation remained our intellectual property. When we listed on Wall Street your father must have deduced that our growth was being built on his work. He was right."

Teresa placed her fingers over her mouth, her eyes wide with shock.

Liam plowed on. "According to my investigator, your father started some sort of legal proceedings against the company, demanding a profit share. My investigator couldn't find any trace of proceedings reaching court so the legal proceedings didn't get very far, because your father ran into trouble with Immigration."

Teresa nodded. "He got deported back to the UK. It happened so fast. I was only six, but I remember. One minute he was there, then gone."

Liam swallowed, hoping he'd be able to get these next words over his tongue. "I think your dad got into trouble with Immigration because my parents put him on their radar. To Dutton and me, it sounds like something someone like him, a Fixer, would do. Your father was trying to sue and they dug into his life and probably found out that his visa was expired or that he was here illegally and they got him hustled out of the country. It's difficult waging a court case in a foreign country when you're not in the country or a citizen of that country. Your credibility is also diminished when you've been deported from said country. It was an easy solution to a very expensive, in their eyes, problem. Dutton also thinks a note in your dad's personnel file at the company was planted. It said he'd taken a leave of absence for a family issue. No one ever questions those so no one asked when he was coming back.

"Did your mom ever talk about your dad?" Liam asked.

Teresa shook her head. "My mom didn't like to deal with anything hard, or inconvenient. If dad was having problems, I doubt he would've shared them with my mom, especially since she was pregnant with Josh at the time." Teresa grimaced. "My mom doesn't handle stress well and he would've tried to protect her."

Liam waited, and watched, as Teresa digested this latest revelation. He watched her beautiful and much-loved face as she stared past him to the sea beyond, her eyes full of sadness. His heart nearly shattered when her eyes glistened with tears.

"I thought he didn't come back because he didn't want to."

"No, he didn't come back because I think they were actively trying to keep him out and then he died in a freak accident." Liam rubbed his forehead with his fingertips. "I am so sorry, Teresa. I am ashamed and mortified and horrified at what they did."

Teresa nodded and didn't say anything and Liam felt cold fingers gripping his heart, about to start that agonizing rip.

"But I'm convinced that's why Linus left you the shares, why he took an interest in you. I think he knew that it was wrong, that he should've treated your father better. He, in his ham-fisted way, tried to right a wrong. And it also explains my mother's antipathy toward you."

Teresa dropped her head to stare at her bare feet and Liam knew that, for as long as he lived, he'd remembered her like this, blond head bowed and her arms wrapped around her waist to comfort herself. He wanted to wrap his arms around her, to hold her as she made sense of this new information, but he didn't think she'd appreciate his touch.

"I don't know what else to say, to tell you how

sorry I am," Liam said, hearing the desperation in his voice. "Again."

Teresa sucked her bottom lip between her teeth and when she released it, he saw the impression they'd left there. Straightening, she lifted her head and Liam couldn't identify all the emotions swimming in and out of her eyes. "I would never have known this if you didn't tell me."

Liam could only nod.

"You know how I feel about you and we could've carried on, had a relationship, and you could've swept this under the carpet, treated it as something that never happened. I wouldn't have had a clue. You had to know that telling me this would put what we have at risk…"

He knew that. God, he was living it! Liam just held her steady gaze and waited for her to continue. It was her turn to speak and his to wait for her verdict.

"Why did you tell me?" Teresa demanded.

Liam knitted his fingers together and squeezed. "Because I didn't want there to be any lies between us. Our pasts, my parents, caused so much trouble, for you—"

"And you."

"They lied and they manipulated and they used and they lied some more," Liam said, his voice rough. "I don't want there to be any more lies between us. And withholding truth is just another form of lying. I'm done with it and I'm done with them and what I thought was normal. Normal is not a cold marriage between two people who were more concerned about money and power and status than the people who worked for them and, to an extent, me. Normal is not a cold, quiet house with no affection and no laughter. Normal is not keeping everything bottled up to the point you think your head might explode. I want normal, Teresa. I want normal so much it hurts."

"And how do you define normal, Liam?" Teresa softly asked.

He had to say this before she walked away, before those fingers tugging on his heart ripped it apart. "Normal is you, with me. Normal would be you and I married, both working at our separate careers, supporting and loving and learning from each other. Normal would be calling you to ask you for input when I have a problem, and vice versa. It's doing the best we can for ourselves, our kids and, I know this sounds corny, the world." He lifted one shoulder, his throat tightening and his eyes burning. "There is nobody I trust more than you, and that now feels normal. Finally, normal is me loving you for as long as I live. But I know that's a long shot."

"Sometimes long shots pay off," Teresa softly said. Liam frowned at her, not sure of her meaning.

"I don't understand."

A small smile tipped her sexy mouth up. "Okay then, what if I just said yes?"

It had been a tough morning, he got that, but he was losing track of this conversation. "Yes to what?"

Teresa touched her tongue to her top lip and Liam's heart stopped at the brilliant blue of her eyes. "Yes to everything. You, me, the work thing, the kids thing.

The marriage thing that has absolutely nothing to do with shares and everything to do with us."

"Uh—"

Teresa leaned forward and placed her hands on his knees. "Are you with me, Liam?" she asked.

Barely. He was pretty sure that joy had just drowned out his ability to speak so he just nodded. But because there was still a kernel of doubt—this was too damn easy!—Liam forced himself to construct a sentence. "Say that again?"

Teresa rubbed his thighs with her thumbs. "I love you, darling. I want to spend every minute of my life with you."

"Are you sure? Did you hear what I said about what my parents did to your dad?"

Teresa nodded. "Yeah, I did. I'm still going to need some time to process that and I will probably never have a relationship with your mother—"

"Completely understandable," Liam jumped in.

"But what they did has nothing to do with us. What they did, what your dad did to try and make amends, brought us together. We triumphed, despite having everything but the kitchen sink thrown at us. I'd be a fool to walk away from a love that stubborn, that persistent."

Liam's fingers touched her cheek. "You really do love me."

"I really do," Teresa said, her lips curving under the pressure of his thumb.

"I love you so much, Teresa," Liam said as she lifted her chin to receive his kiss. He wanted to dive into her, to lose himself in her and her warmth and beauty and love but there were one or two issues that still needed to be cleared up. "Going forward, can we agree on a couple of things?"

Teresa lifted her eyebrows. "What things?"

"First, can we remove the contact numbers for any and all Fixers from our phones? From now on, we live exceptionally boring lives that don't require the dubious talents of men with connections to pave the way for us."

Teresa nodded, her eyes sparkling. "That's a great idea. What else?"

"Will you marry me, as soon as possible?" Liam asked. "Like within the month?"

Teresa looked at him as she considered his question. "Liam, you know how long it takes to organize a wedding. Yeah, I managed to do Brooks and Nic's in record time but it nearly killed me."

Dammit, he was going to have to wait. But it was a long shot anyway. "Okay, two months? Three?"

Teresa smiled. "How about three days, on a beach at sunset? That'll give our friends enough time to get here. We won't invite Catherine but we will invite your biological dad and his family. How does that sound?"

Liam knew that he was doing his best goldfish look. "But you are a wedding planner. I thought you'd want a fairy-tale wedding."

Teresa's mouth was soft against his. "Liam, you are my fairy tale. I don't need anything else." She kissed him again and pulled back to hold his face. "Shall I meet you on the beach in three days' time?"

"Anywhere you are is where I want to be," Liam said, hauling her into his arms.

Epilogue

Teresa rather liked the way that Liam's eyes kept returning to her leg and she deliberately toyed with the ruffle that ended very high up on her left thigh. She knew that, with the smallest hint, his hand would be under the asymmetrical folds of her ball gown and heading north.

She rather liked his hand there and welcomed his touch day or night but they were on their way to the first of what they hoped would be a yearly event—the Christopher Ball—and she'd spent a fortune on this hand-beaded gown.

Liam squinted at her as their limousine moved slowly through the traffic to the red carpet. "Is it just me being romantic or does that gown look a little wedding-y?"

Teresa wasn't surprised he'd noticed. Her husband was ridiculously astute.

On hearing that she was to marry at such short notice, Corinne, brilliant friend and personal assistant that she was, found her a rose-patterned lace dress, with spaghetti straps and a fitted bodice. It was a perfect dress for a perfect beach ceremony witnessed by Matt and Nadia, Liam's fantastic new family, Joshua and a handful of friends who could rearrange their schedule on short notice. As wonderful as the ceremony and the joyous dinner afterward was, she'd still yearned for a one-off designer gown, something utterly extravagant. This ball that she and Nic conceived was the perfect opportunity to have something designed that was utterly unique and breathtaking.

Her off-the-shoulder, backless dress with its hand-beaded bodice and frilled skirt bordered on the edges of being bridal but Teresa didn't care. As the wife of Seattle's most influential man, hell, as Teresa St. Claire-Christopher, she didn't give a hoot. Liam loved it and that was all that mattered.

"You look beautiful. I'm so lucky to have married you," Liam murmured.

Teresa, not caring about her lipstick, leaned forward to receive his kiss. "Glad you like the dress."

"I love it. But as always, it would look so much better on the floor," Liam commented, making Teresa smile. Yeah, no. This was a twenty-thousand-dollar dress; the only place it was going was back in its plastic bag and back into her walk-in closet.

The limousine stopped. "We're here."

Teresa looked out the tinted windows and saw Nicolette standing on the red carpet, and behind her, and behind barriers, were the photographers, cameras already pointed their way. Nic looked fantastic in a long, red boho-inspired ball gown. She was talking to the camera, and Teresa wondered where Brooks was, knowing that he couldn't be that far away. Nic lowered her mic, handed it off to someone and headed for their limo. Liam opened the door for her and Teresa scooted up so that Nic could sit down next to her. Kissing Teresa's cheek, she took the bottle of Evian Liam handed her and took a grateful sip.

"Wow, this is hard work."

Teresa cocked her head. Nic was looking a bit tired and pale. "Are you okay? I know how hard you've been working, helping me to arrange this ball—"

"It was the least I could do since it's raising funds for our foundation."

A couple of months after their wedding, Brooks and Nic set up a foundation to raise funds for the prevention of human trafficking and, on hearing about it, Teresa immediately wanted to arrange an event to raise funds for the cause very dear to Nic's heart. Her film was also premiering tonight and Teresa knew she was as nervous as hell. Add that to her covering the event for her day job, Teresa understood that Nic was burning the candle at both ends.

"Where's Brooks?"

"Inside. Raising money for us." Nic softly smiled and when she touched her stomach Teresa knew exactly why she was so tired.

"Oh my God, when?" she cried, wrapping both her arms around Nic's shoulders.

"It's new so not for a long time," Nic said, grinning.

"What's going on?" Liam asked, confused.

"Nic's pregnant!" Teresa told him, ecstatic for her friend. She and Liam weren't quite ready for kids but they were having a bunch of fun practicing how to make one. "What does Brooks think? Was it planned? Are you going to find out the sex?"

Nic laughed at her questions. "You and I are going to have a long lunch and we'll discuss this to death but right now we need to get to work."

"But this is so exciting!" Teresa said, clasping her hands. "You're happy, all our friends are happy and I love that!"

"I just heard you're planning Shane and Isabel's wedding. Isabel told me that she loved your proposal and now that The Opulence is reopened, it seems perfect for their wedding," Nicolette told her.

Teresa clapped her hands in delight. "Yay!" Then she mock-pouted. "I'm still a bit cross with Jessie and Gideon for eloping."

"They both made huge donations to this event and Jessie is performing for free so you have to forgive them," Liam reminded her, laughter in his gorgeous eyes.

Teresa winked at him. "Maybe. Okay, let's get this done."

Nic nodded and glanced at the discreet bangle watch on her wrist. "Give me a few minutes, and we're going to live-feed your arrival. I'll give the signal to your driver when we are live."

Nic slipped out of the car and the door shut behind them. Teresa turned to Liam and her smile faded at his serious face. "What's wrong? What's the matter?" she demanded, placing her hand on his thigh.

Liam shook his head as he pulled a folded piece of paper out of his tuxedo jacket. "Do you know that six months has passed and in another six months you can divest yourself of your shares in Christopher Corporation?"

Time flew when you were happy. Teresa shrugged as she took the paper he held out. "I was thinking about keeping those shares for our kids."

"I love that idea," Liam told her. He nodded at the paper. "That was delivered by Linus's lawyer this morning. It's a letter from my…dad. Linus." Teresa caught the look he sent toward the entrance of the venue and saw the guilt on his face. He and John had become exceptionally close these past few months and she knew that he battled with the idea that he'd never been close to Linus. "Read it…"

Teresa slowly opened the letter.

Liam,
I've never been a great one for writing letters and I'm even worse at love letters. But in its way, this is one, and it's the best I can do.
  I was always proud of you, proud to call you mine. No matter what you hear, what you discover, I wanted you to know that.

I'm sorry I never warned you about giving Teresa the company shares. I have no idea what she will do with them when the year is up. I hope they remain in Christopher hands but I can't control that. Giving Teresa the shares was my way of making up for a grievous error in my past. I also like the girl, very much. In my more fanciful moments, I think she'd be an excellent daughter-in-law.

But I'm not there and you know your own mind and I trust your choices. With the company, and more important, for your own happiness.

For God's sake, be happy in love, son. It's all that matters.
Dad

Teresa folded the letter and handed it back to him. She arched an eyebrow. "Are you happy, darling?"

Liam's driver opened the heavy door and the sound of the excited, noisy crowd rushed toward them. But Liam's eyes were steady on her face. "Exceptionally. You?"

"Indescribably. But Liam?"

"Yeah?"

Teresa waved her finger in the direction of her chest. "This dress, seriously, it can't end up on the floor."

Her husband helped her out of the car and sent her a rakish smile. "Oh, but we both know it will."

* * * * *

Don't miss a single episode in the Dynasties:
Secrets of the A-List quartet!

Book One
Tempted by Scandal *by Karen Booth*

Book Two
Taken by Storm *by Cat Schield*

Book Three
Seduced by Second Chances *by Reese Ryan*

Book Four
Redeemed by Passion *by Joss Wood*

COMING NEXT MONTH FROM

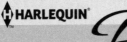

HARLEQUIN

Desire

Available September 3, 2019

#2683 TEXAS-SIZED SCANDAL
Texas Cattleman's Club: Houston • by Katherine Garbera
Houston philanthropist Melinda Perry always played by the rules. Getting pregnant by a mob boss's son was certainly never in the playbook—until now. Can they contain the fallout...and maybe even turn their forbidden affair into forever?

#2684 STRANDED AND SEDUCED
Boone Brothers of Texas • by Charlene Sands
To keep her distance from ex-fling Risk Boone, April Adams pretends to be engaged. But when a storm strands them together and the rich rancher has an accident resulting in amnesia, he suddenly thinks he's the fiancé! Especially when passion overtakes them...

#2685 BLACK TIE BILLIONAIRE
Blackout Billionaires • by Naima Simone
CEO Gideon Knight demands that Shay Neal be his fake fiancée to avenge his family. Too bad he doesn't realize they already shared an anonymous night during the Chicago blackout! But even through the deception, the truth of their chemistry cannot be denied.

#2686 CALIFORNIA SECRETS
Two Brothers • by Jules Bennett
Ethan Michaels is on a mission to reclaim the resort his mother built. Then he's sidetracked by sexy Harper Williams—only to find out she's his enemy's daughter. All's fair in love and war...until Harper's next explosive secret shakes Ethan to his core.

#2687 A BET WITH BENEFITS
The Eden Empire • by Karen Booth
Entrepreneur Mindy Eden scoffs when her sisters bet she can't spend time with her real estate mogul ex without succumbing to temptation. But it soon becomes crystal clear that second chances are in the cards. Will Mindy risk her business for one more shot at pleasure?

#2688 POWER PLAY
The Serenghetti Brothers • by Anna DePalo
Hockey legend and sports industry tycoon Jordan Serenghetti needs his injury healed—and fast. Too bad he clashes with his physical therapist over a kiss they once shared—and Jordan forgot! As passions flare, will she be ready for more revelations from his player past?

Get 4 FREE REWARDS!

We'll send you 2 FREE Books
plus 2 FREE Mystery Gifts.

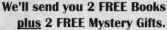

Harlequin® Desire books feature heroes who have it all: wealth, status, incredible good looks... everything but the right woman.

FREE Value Over **$20**

She curled her hands into fists, grabbing hold of his T-shirt.
And she had no idea what the hell was running through her
head as she stood there looking up into those wildly blue
eyes, the present moment mingling with memories of that
night long ago.

While he witnessed the deepest, darkest thing she'd ever
gone through. Something no one else even knew about.

He was the only one who knew.

The only one who knew what had started everything.
Olivia didn't understand. Her parents didn't understand.
And they had never wanted to understand.

But he knew. He knew and he had already seen what a
disaster she was.

There was no facade to protect. No new enlightened
sense of who she was. No narrative about her as a lost cause
out there roaming the world.

He'd already seen her break apart. For real. Not the
Vanessa that existed when she was hiding. Hiding her
problems from her family. Hiding her feelings behind a high.

Hiding. And more hiding.

No. He had seen her at her lowest when she hadn't been able to hide.

And somehow, he seemed to bring that out in her. Because she wasn't able to hide her anger.

And she wasn't able to hide this. Whatever the wildness was that was coursing through her veins. No, she couldn't hide that either. And she wasn't sure she cared.

So she was just going to let the wildness carry her forward.

She couldn't remember the last time she had done that. The last time she'd allowed herself this pure kind of over-the-top emotion.

It had been pain. The pain she felt that night she lost the baby. That was the last time she had let it all go. In all the time since then when she had been on the verge of being overwhelmed by emotion she had crushed it completely. Hidden it beneath drugs. Hidden it beneath therapy speak.

She had carefully kept herself in hand since she'd gotten sober. Kept herself under control.

What she hadn't allowed herself to do was feel.

She was feeling now. And she wasn't going to stop it.

She launched herself forward, and her lips connected with his.

And before she knew it, she was kissing Jacob Dalton with all the passion she hadn't known existed inside of her.

Don't miss
Lone Wolf Cowboy *by Maisey Yates,*
available August 2019 wherever
Harlequin® books and ebooks are sold.

www.Harlequin.com

PHMYEXP0819

"To answer your other question," he murmured. "Why did I
single you out? Your first guess was correct. Because you are
so beautiful I couldn't help following you around this over-
the-top ballroom filled with people who possess more money
than sense. The women here can't outshine you. They're like
peacocks, spreading their plumage, desperate to be noticed,
and here you are among them, like the moon. Bright, alone,
above it all and eclipsing every one of them. What I don't
understand is how no one else noticed before me. Why every
man in this place isn't standing behind me in a line just for
the chance to be near you."

Silence swelled around them like a bubble, muting the din
of the gala. His words seemed to echo in the cocoon, and he
marveled at them. Hadn't he sworn he didn't do pretty words?
Yet it had been him talking about peacocks and moons.

What was she doing to him?

Even as the question echoed in his mind, her head tilted
back and she stared at him, her lovely eyes darker…hotter. In

that moment, he'd stand under a damn balcony and serenade her if she continued looking at him like that. He curled his fingers into his palm, reminding himself with the pain that he couldn't touch her. Still, the only sound that reached his ears was the quick, soft pants breaking on her pretty lips.

"I—I need to go," she whispered, already shifting back and away from him. "I—" She didn't finish the thought, but turned and waded into the crowd, distancing herself from him.

He didn't follow; she hadn't said no, but she hadn't said yes, either. And though he'd caught the desire in her gaze—his stomach still ached from the gut punch of it—she had to come to him.

Or ask him to come for her.

Rooted where she'd left him, he tracked her movements.

Saw the moment she cleared the mass of people and strode in the direction of the double doors where more tray-bearing staff emerged and exited.

Saw when she paused, palm pressed to one of the panels.

Saw when she glanced over her shoulder in his direction.

Even across the distance of the ballroom, the electric shock of that look whipped through him, sizzled in his veins. Moments later, she disappeared from view. Didn't matter; his feet were already moving in her direction.

That glance, that look. It'd sealed her fate.

Sealed it for both of them.

What will happen when these two find each other alone during the blackout?

Find out in
Black Tie Billionaire
by USA TODAY *bestselling author Naima Simone available September 2019 wherever Harlequin® Desire books and ebooks are sold.*

www.Harlequin.com

Want to give in to temptation with
steamy tales of irresistible desire?

Check out **Harlequin® Presents®,
Harlequin® Desire** and
Harlequin® Kimani™ Romance books!

New books available every month!

CONNECT WITH US AT:

Facebook.com/groups/HarlequinConnection

 Facebook.com/HarlequinBooks

 Twitter.com/HarlequinBooks

 Instagram.com/HarlequinBooks

 Pinterest.com/HarlequinBooks

ReaderService.com

**ROMANCE WHEN
YOU NEED IT**

PGENRE2018